The Last Cathar

Kate Riley

Published by
Melange Books, LLC
White Bear Lake, MN 55110
www.melange-books.com

Cover Art by Lynsee Lauritsen

To my daughters, Erin, Gigi and Jesse
who always thought I could

Prologue

"Caedite eos. Novit enim Dominus qui sunt eius.
Kill them all, God will recognize his own."

Béziers, Languedoc region, Southern France
July 1209

Beranger Serras wearily prodded his mule farther along an isolated path, then, stopped at a slight opening around a bend. Parched and eager for a bit of respite from the heat, he slowly eased himself down, leaving the tired animal to nibble on a scarce patch of green. He winced as he rubbed his lower back, then pulled out a small leather flask from his pack, twisted off the plug and tilted back the last few drops of water. Closing his eyes, he savored every drop.

Wiping the sweat off his upper lip with the back of his hand, he edged closer to the cliff for a better view and swung his palm over his brow to shade his eyes from the sun. This made it easier to survey the vista before him. From the height of his mountain perch, the scorched, yellow scrub that sprawled across the stony land below was testament to the summer's sweltering heat. The worst he had seen in years. But what he saw next sent shivers crawling up his spine.

In the far distance, long strings of barges jammed the great River Orb, while gaps in the forest canopy revealed a steady dark thread of marching troupes. Like an endless procession of foraging ants, the Crusader army twisted and wound its way along the dusty, ancient roads that led to the city of Béziers. His home.

1

Even though a group of that size could only move at a snail's pace, he estimated that the army would reach the city in a day or so, and he felt an urgency to get back as quickly as possible. He pursed his lips and let out a long sigh. What lay before him explained the anxious feeling that had shadowed him all the way from Toulouse. The devil was on his way.

He knew, for the most part, this was about power, land and faith. Catharism was growing, and the number of Believers had become a dangerous challenge to the policies of Rome, as well as the French kings who both felt their power was being eroded.

He shook his head in frustration. He and his fellow Believers were simple Gnostic, spiritual people, no matter what their occupation or rank. Their "crime" was that their arcane knowledge of the bloodlines of Jesus and the Mary Magdalene was in direct conflict with the Church's propaganda of the Crucifixion.

To a few knowledgeable men in Rome, however, there was something far more desirable than the eradication of a heretic faith. They were obviously aware of the Cathars' sacred guardianship. He suspected they might even know the identity of the man entrusted with knowledge of where the great treasure was safely hidden. To this desperate and fanatical Church, the only one solution was to find the treasure and then kill them all.

He nervously wiped his brow one more time, mounted and booted his plodding mule to hurry onward through the dusty, parched landscape. The journey he had taken was long, especially at his age, but he was grateful that he had been prudent. What had been in his care was now in another's safe hands.

* * * *

As he arrived through the gates, it was easy to see that in the months of his absence the town had filled with residents from the surrounding areas. All were preparing themselves for what they felt would likely be just another siege.

They were no strangers to these tactics, and a sense of camaraderie was in the air. Animals that had not been slaughtered were being led inside the city's protective walls, while its citizens dug trenches and took in supplies. The town was alive with the sounds of hammering, of stones being piled up, and of food being stored. Small boys excitedly feigned death in swordplay as dogs barked and younger children threw sticks and stones at imagined enemies.

"Ah, Beranger! You have finally returned! Just in time my friend." He turned to see a familiar face, Johan, a local blacksmith, walking towards him. Holding a hammer in one hand and slapping Beranger on the back with the other, he tipped his head to one side.

"Look quickly to your left. The old Bishop from Montpellier has ridden on ahead to negotiate with all of us good citizens and heretics of Béziers. Shall we follow and see what terms we are to be offered this time?"

Beranger turned to see an obese old monk nervously clasping the pummel for balance as he booted his sweat-laden mule through the city's fortified gates. His unfortunate animal brayed under the strain of the monk's wide girth. No formal announcements about who he was and why he was there would be needed. Word of mouth was swift enough in these situations. He turned back to his friend.

"I've seen the army, Johan. It's unusually large. I have a bad feeling about this business. Let's go quickly. I'll leave my mule at your shed. There's sure to be a crowd, and I want to make my way to the front. I want to hear with my own ears what the Bishop has to say."

First in small groups and then en mass, the crowd began to follow the Bishop towards the Cathedral. The town consuls were summoned, and a public meeting was quickly called. By the time the consuls arrived, the Cathedral was already filled to capacity. Throngs of onlookers filled the doorways and vestibules, spilling outside into the street, desperate to hear the conversation.

Beranger managed to squeeze through to the front, losing Johan to the crowd in the back. The heat and stench from so many packed, unwashed bodies was rank, and as he struggled to breathe in the heavy air, rivulets of sweat dribbled down his back.

The old Bishop wiped his brow and took a deep breath. All eyes were upon him as he spoke loudly.

"Citizens of Béziers, I am here in good faith and as God's messenger to advise you to surrender. The crusading army is massive; its strength is unbeatable. You cannot win this battle, nor is it for many of you, *your* battle to fight. The terms are straightforward. If those of the true faith of Rome, that is to say, our Catholic brothers and sisters, are prepared to deliver known heretics into the legate's hands, their lives and property will be respected and spared."

Beranger watched as a wave of angry outcries from the consuls drowned out any further plea from the bishop. As his words echoed back through the crowd, it exploded into a sea of enraged fists and defiant shouts.

The old bishop fearfully looked around as the ugly crowd shouted insults that were growing personal and deadly. Shouting as best he could over the noise, he pleaded to his fellow Catholics.

"I am begging you to save your lives and the lives of your wives and children. Leave Béziers in peace and abandon these heretics to their fate. This insidious evil has rooted too deeply in this city of Satan."

As he expected, his terms fell on deaf ears. The consul members, having heard enough, did not need time to reach a decision. A big man with broad shoulders stood up. In a deep, loud voice that all could hear, he declared to the Bishop that he spoke for all. At this, a hush came over the anxious crowd as every ear listened to his words.

"Leave our city in peace old man, and take these words to the Pope's henchmen. We would rather be drowned in the salt sea's brine than surrender or betray our fellow citizens. No one will have so much as a brass farthing from us at the price of a change of allegiance."

The crowd went wild. Shouts of *partage* and honor swept like a wave through the crowd. A siege it would be. These crusaders and their bloated army would see what the Bitterois were made of. The name itself echoed the ancient Roman courage that coursed through their veins. The crowd dispersed and with renewed and determined vigor returned to the business of fortifying its city. Beranger returned to his home and prepared his soul for what might be his last days.

No matter how confident his fellow citizens felt, Beranger could not shake the ominous feeling of foreboding danger.

* * * *

Jean de Beynac, a crusading knight, couldn't have asked for a better situation. This Crusade was a Godsend. After completing his obligatory

40 days, he could easily return home with booty in hand and coffers replenished, all for doing his duty to God and to the Church. Whoever killed a Cathar was given an indulgence worth two years' penance and the protection of the Church as a crusader. The real pearl was that all of this could be accomplished without the bother and expense of ships and tedious travel to foreign lands.

He had, however, recently received an order from the Papal Legate that suggested a far bigger prize might be his for the taking, a prize held by a Cathar named Beranger Serras. Beynac had already traveled these lands years ago in his youth and was well aware of the secret treasure of the Cathars. There would be only one reason why the Vatican had ordered him to find and bring this man back alive. His identity, they said, would be proven by a certain mark on his body. Beynac was no fool. Should Serras disclose his secrets to him before an unfortunate "accident," his future would be ensured.

Restraining his horse from nibbling on some parched grass, he indulged himself in the delicious knowledge of the untold power and riches that were at stake, not only for him but for his descendants. He meant all of it to be his.

* * * *

Early the next morning preparations at the camp continued: Troops lit campfires and settled down to a breakfast of stale bread and thin gruel. Garrison commanders were busy organizing their defense posts. The crusader generals were working out plans for their first assault. The army was at least a few days away from any attack, and the mood was casual. Chanting monks droned on over the sound of braying mules and barking dogs, as lifeless silk banners wilted in the already stifling heat.

Jean and a few of his comrades rode toward the city walls. Keeping a respectable distance from the ramparts, they trotted around surveying them for flaws. He grunted, satisfied with his assessment. The siege experts would have no choice now but to concede that, indeed, he was correct. Breaching the walls would be difficult. As the meeting convened, he let out a bored, vindicated sigh and rode off, leaving the others to finish their tasks. He had something far more important to deal with. He had to ensure that a certain Beranger Serras was his and his alone. The opportunity would come sooner than he expected.

* * * *

Within hours, a handful of young camp stragglers got into a row with a small group of Béziers' youth who watched over the city's protective walls. As the crusader ruffians loudly taunted them, the Bitterois hurled back their own slurs with a vengeance. Excitement was high, and the Béziers' youth were over-confident from the safety of their protected position. They decided to show the crusader scum what they were made of. Gathering coarse banners, spears, sticks, and a few drums, they swung open the gate and charged noisily down the slope to the river, shouting at the top of their voices. Mayhem ensued.

Suddenly realizing they had an incredible opportunity, the crusaders shouted at once: "Attack! The gates are open!"

Citizens peering over the walls screamed and cheered as their young men, outnumbered and exposed, fought their way back to the rampart and up the slope. But the real prize was the open gate, and the mercenaries quickly shoved and pounded their way through it into the city itself. Deserting their posts, many young Bitterois descended to the streets to join the brawl, leaving the crusaders free to prop their scaling ladders against the unguarded walls. The town was now wide open to its enemy.

Young crusader squires ran to dress their knights and their war-horses, while the indignant knights, furious at being caught off guard, rushed to make sure they were the first to begin plundering. Bloodlust and a frenzy for loot coursed through their veins; they would be dammed before they would let camp stragglers get their filthy paws on any of it.

The crusaders showed no mercy as the Biterrois fell back through the narrow streets. The city streets were alive with the metallic clashes of arms, war-whoops of the attacking knights and the dying howls of men, women and children.

Bells of the city began to ring out the alarm, as thousands of panic-stricken men, women and children crowded into the Cathedral of St. Mary Magdalene and other churches all over the town.

More than fifteen hundred terrified, weeping Cathar and Catholic people were inside the cathedral when the crusaders forced open the doors and charged the congregation. Amidst screams of terror and shrieks of the wounded, their broadswords slashed and stabbed indiscriminately as their victims clung to their children, husbands, wives, reliquaries and crucifixes until no one within was left standing. Having accomplished their slaughter, they set fire to the cathedral and then turned their attention to gathering material wealth. It was a scene of death and destruction that was repeated all over Beziers.

Monks had no time to sing the 'Te Deum' because during that one afternoon everyone in the town, from ancient Cathar to newborn Catholic baby, was being put to the sword.

* * * *

Jean de Beynac charged through the gates, his cudgel tossing any mercenaries aside. The streets were filling with routiers rampaging through the town, kicking in doors, pillaging, killing and raping. All but the most costly household objects were scornfully tossed into the streets. He watched with morbid interest as an old priest limped down the street, cross held high in his hands, begging to intercede for the lives of the women and children. When he turned to look again, the man had been dragged by his white hair and piteously bludgeoned to death.

Intent only on his prize, Jean navigated his horse carefully, sidestepping through a multitude of bloodied, torn bodies, towards a single, small dwelling at the north end of the city. He prayed that he would not be too late.

As he arrived at his destination, his anger rose. The front door hung haphazardly, and a pile of useless, bloodied household contents lay strewn about. Dismounting in one stride, he booted the door open, but it appeared that he was too late. A lifeless, bloodied body lay on the floor.

"Damn to hell," Beynac growled, then spat bitterly.

Looking around at the broken furniture and household goods, he could tell that the man had fought bravely. Striding over to the body, Beynac leaned over, grabbed his shirt and pulled it open to reveal the mark that he suspected he would find on his shoulder. It was him all right--Berenger Serras, the warrior known only as *the Keeper* who guarded the Cathar treasure. And some damn idiot had stupidly killed his

7

opportunity for fortune and power. And over what? A bit of pewter? No one else would have known the importance of this man.

Suddenly he heard a desperate gasp for air. *Could it be? Was it possible?*

On bended knee, he gently rolled Beranger onto his back and leaned closer to his bloody chest. A shallow breath confirmed that his prey was still alive, but not by much. He smiled at his luck. As Beranger painfully opened his eyes, Jean could barely contain his frustration to remain calm. The man was obviously on death's door, and this would be his only chance to get the information he wanted. He smiled for dramatic effect, then, spoke as gently as he could.

"Beranger Serras, Jean de Beynac at your service. I am in a position to help you. In fact, my friend, I suspect we could help each other. I am a great believer in your faith, and God as my witness, I only wish to help. If you need me to share a message, or perhaps deliver something of importance, I would be honored to carry on your most noble mission."

Beranger weakly moaned a reply, but it was so low that Jean could not hear. In truth, if he could have strangled the bastard into talking he would have, but thinking that Berenger was about to entrust him with his secret, he gently held his hand, smiled again and prompted him to repeat what he had said. "You can trust me. I am a friend."

The next few moments would be seared into his memory for the rest of his life. Beranger's broken body took on a soft golden glow as if it had a burning lamp within. The light intensified and grew stronger until it lit up the area around him. Startled, Jean tried to drop his hand and move away, but Beranger held on with a vice-like grip. Suddenly his eyes opened wide and he stared directly at Jean. His voice boomed with authority from an unknown source of strength.

"Fool! Do you not think I see through your lies? Hear me well, Jean de Beynac. Searching for the Cathar treasure will cost you in ways that you cannot predict. Your dark soul will never know peace, and your coffers will fill only with sand and wind. What you seek is already safely with another, so kill me if you must, but I will die in peace knowing that the treasure is safe from the likes of you."

Jean's face hardened with anger and frustration. He gripped Beranger's neck with his other hand and choked out his vengeance. "Go ahead and die old man. I'll spend the rest of my life, if need be, finding the next Keeper. The treasure will be mine!"

Beranger faltered for a moment and then fixed his gaze on Jean. Blood foamed and trickled from his mouth, as he spoke his final words. "Jean de Beynac, the treasure will never be yours, and this I promise. Ten years to this day, at this very hour, I will return and live long enough to protect the treasure from your last cursed descendent."

Beranger's eyes closed. There was a whoosh of air, and as suddenly as the glow had begun, it went out. He took one last gasp and was gone.

Frustrated, Jean rose, swore and smashed his fist into a broken cupboard door. Curse be dammed. Heretical, nonsensical beliefs of reincarnation needed to be stopped, and if these heretics could not see their way to salvation through the church, then they deserved to die. He looked around and gave a hefty boot to Beranger's still body. There would be nothing of importance here. In a deadly mood, he headed towards the more affluent area of town where he would do whatever he needed to refill his coffers or relieve his frustration. This land and its people were already dead.

* * * *

Ten years to the day, and indeed at the precise hour predicted, a very special child was born in the nearby city of Toulouse. According to Cathar faith, it was the custom to welcome a new baby as one would welcome an adult who had just returned from a long journey. There was no standard prayer for this moment, only a time-honored acknowledgement of the child's past existence before it was completely forgotten in the haze of rebirth. As Olivier Serras lovingly gazed at his newborn daughter, their eyes locked in the unconditional love of that moment.

But as he began to speak, he gasped in amazement. The eyes that looked back at him were not the eyes of his baby girl, but a direct window into the soul of a strong warrior. They drew him in, demanding to be recognized, their strength speaking of lifetimes of courage and ancient wisdom. Suddenly, he knew this soul had come for a singular purpose. This would be no ordinary daughter, but a woman with extraordinary courage. In that moment of exchange, he panicked and

9

almost lost his hold on the babe. But a heartbeat later, she was once again his little girl who began to fuss for the security of her mother's breast and the warm milk it provided. After much deliberation, they named her India, honored Cathar granddaughter of Beranger Serras.

Chapter One

Carcassonne, Languedoc
1290

India Serras' daily vigil of spying on the crowds below never altered, never wavered, her routine tailored completely to the task at hand. Her sparsely furnished room, comfortable enough for her intent, was well placed on the second floor because the borders of her casement window looked over the main market-square. With gimlet eye, she scanned the street below, the summer breeze subtly stirring, slowly swirling in response to her gaze. She missed nothing. Not a single movement went unnoticed, for from the confines of her towered keep, India was the reliquary of a remarkable secret.

She was a tiny woman, almost childlike in size, a factor which years ago had strongly determined her survival. Now into her seventies, she was no more than a wisp of her former diminutive self. A coarse brown woolen tunic, a relic from another age, scratched at her parched, dry skin, and her thin, white hair barely covered her head. Rogue bristles sprouted from her chin and ugly brown spots covered her arms and gnarled hands. Old age had not been kind.

Her solitary chair was strategically poised for her covert observations of the narrow streets of Carcassonne, as she impatiently waited and watched for a man she had never met and would not recognize. India believed that the world beyond the borders of her window was drawn to her, like a grand play cast for her own purpose. The main character would enter her stage through a bond they shared, a tale that had begun long before her time. Daily she willed him to arrive

11

before it was too late.

Her maidservant, Favia, a sullen young chit only just into womanhood, pouted her way into the room and began the daily, perfunctory task of delousing India's clothes and hair. The old woman resented depending on anyone, least of all a servant girl who didn't know her place. However, the girl's quick fingers and young eyes were far better suited to this task. She sniffed and then shifted her weight to compensate for the interruption. Her body language and pursed lips would be statement enough that she wasn't in the mood to listen to Favia's regular litany of household complaints.

"I'll be off to the market after this, Madame. We're in need of some garlic and a cabbage. I won't be long."

"See that you're not. Don't think I don't know how you spill tales like water from a bucket for anyone to listen," India replied gruffly.

It was a tight rope she walked with that girl. She didn't understand why Favia must ask so many questions or why she couldn't seem to do anything right. Taking a deep breath, and rethinking her tone, she softened a little lest Favia repeat her usual retaliatory silent treatment when she returned. "Get yourself a sugar stick if you've a fancy for one. Just don't dawdle." India kept staring out the window, maintaining air of boredom as her servant's nimble fingers worked away through her scalp and clothes. The only sound was of cracked nits and the market below.

Nodding at the completion of her task, Favia sucked her thumb, purpled by the blood of squashed lice from her mistress's head, and then clogged her way down the wooden steps. When she had left, India tugged her shawl tighter and then shifted herself forward straining to see her servant head towards the vegetable stalls until she was lost in a sea of color and noise. She was, as she rightly suspected, the subject of much idle gossip by her servant. This, alone, was a dangerous business, and it vexed her sorely that the little idiot's prattle could be her undoing. Should her words reach the long ears of the clergy, the cost would be so much more than an old woman's aged body.

The frustrating irony was that she relied on her gossip to know what was going on in town, and Favia knew it. More than once, she had returned from the market, petulant and silent, knowing full well that her locked lips were an excellent retaliation to India's cross words.

The streets of Carcassonne were filled these days with fair-bound merchants and pilgrims on their way to Rome. The Hot Fair was soon to begin, and thousands arrived almost daily now, causing the already crowded, narrow streets to be even more congested. The market's tantalizing aromas of roasted meats sizzling over smoking fires and freshly baked bread mingled with the foul stench of excrement, rotting garbage, unwashed bodies and urine-soaked muck.

As she watched the pilgrims in their muddied brown mantles plod staff in hand into the city, it was not hard to separate merchant from Palmer. The latter came heavily laden, limping into the city holding onto others for support. The palm fronds in hand were a sure sign that they had undertaken a pilgrimage and were returning from the Holy Land. Some came on horseback, others in carts piled high with their belongings, but all wore the distinctive scallop shell. She cackled knowingly to herself. They would be lucky to make their destination at all, for before reaching the warm cypresses of Italy, they would die of old age, disease, or have their throats slit by robbers. Only the ragged "fortunate" few would get to lay their offerings at Peter's Tomb for the clergy to rake in like hay and send to the Pope. The sweet irony of it all was that most of the money would no doubt pay for his Holiness's most recent obsession, a young Venetian courtesan named Cecile. Or, as the commoners liked to call her, "The Pope's whore." Yet, still they came, paying their way to Heaven.

What his Holiness himself wouldn't pay to get his hands on what I've hidden.

The usual clamor was even louder as the local merchants, whores and thieves took advantage of the moneyed out-of-towners. Merchants in rough woolen tunics, their legs and faces weathered brown from exposure, bellowed out their wares. Tradesmen shouted against each other to attract customers. Squealing pigs, squawking chickens, and the clop, clop, clop of hooves were a never-ending din echoing their way to her window.

Would he arrive today? Was he in this crowd? India scanned faces, dress, carriage. A solitary man stood out in the crowd, his stance strong, his crimson cape the quality and color of a nobleman. He seemed to be finding his bearings, and she wondered, as she had over and over again

13

for more than four decades, if he could be looking for her. Was he friend or foe? As his hand covered his eyes from the sun, he squinted in her direction. Her heart skipped a beat. Her gaze stalked his every move as he slowly sauntered from stall to stall. Finally settling on one, he flipped a coin to a pretty young thing and grabbed an apple not inches from her breast.

The fat, older woman beside her slapped the coin from the smiling girl's hand then scowled a warning. "Cheeky rogue! The coin is for the apple, not my daughter!"

Hat in hand, the stranger dipped his head, slipped a wink to the girl, and tossed his prize into the air, catching it with a flourish. However, before he could take a bite, he smiled and walked towards another man, slapping his shoulder in greeting. As they walked away, India's hope followed.

"It's not him," India muttered. "Not him. Again." She sighed. Years of lying, hiding, pretending, weighed heavily on her soul.

She squinted, the better to see the faces below. A bailiff wielding a thick staff chased a scrawny youth in pursuit of his stolen goods, while a herd of goats, driven by a ragged hide-covered shepherd, caused a cart to spill over and tempers along with it. Ladies, nobles and their entourage, jostling shoulder to shoulder with broad-faced peasants, sidestepped to avoid the argument and donkey shite.

She wondered aloud if she'd been prudent to leave things this close, for the tale and its telling must be passed on for safekeeping. Her sight had been steadily failing for several years, and old age was catching up in other frustrating ways. Each day presented her with new aches and pains and the never-ending need for sleep. The dizzy spells were becoming more frequent, more frightening, and only last month she had survived a mighty pain in her chest. But burning memories and sheer determination had gotten her this far, and she would see it through to the end. She owed the others that much at least.

It was hard to find a moment without pain in her memories, but they were there, moments of pure joy, moments free of fear. She must remember everything while she could—like the way her feet stepped lightly over moss-covered rocks or the coolness of hard ground as she padded along the hidden trails, dense woods guarding her way. She

14

sighed, remembering the feel of her bare feet on meadow grasses.

In her next life, she thought, she would walk that path again, morning dew clinging to the forest leaves that would kiss her face. The intoxicating smell of damp earth would penetrate her very being, and the morning's soft mist would embrace her, awaken her memory and whisper that it still remembered her name.

For years, she had hoped that a familiar name might tumble from a weary mouth, but she had long since given up hope and had stopped asking. Just how long had it been? Ten? Twenty? No, it had to be at least thirty years since she had even seen someone she recognized. As she strained for lost images in the back corners of her mind, fragments of long forgotten memories began to filter through. It was the summer before her hip began to give her so much trouble, and she had been at the market trying to sort through the best of a cartload of wilted, old cabbages. She turned to watch a commotion that centered on a large, unruly crowd coming her way.

A little nervous, she watched as the loud taunting and jeering preceded five or six scruffy young lads as they pushed and poked a hollowed-eyed, tattered old woman. Their prey, whose mind had long-since wandered away, shuffled mindlessly through the growing crowd. India's heart beat in sympathy for the unfortunate soul, as people either jumped out of the beggar's way or joined in with obscenities and spitting. It was then that she noticed *las debanadoras,* the large yellow cross of a heretic sewn onto the woman's breast, and recognized the face from her past. Although covered in sores and gaunt from starvation, there was no doubt that this was Guillemette, the weaver's wife.

India had heard that given the choice between recanting and a burning pyre she had chosen to spend her days as a repentant Christian. This decision was made as her husband and children were burned at the stake. No wonder she had lost her mind.

Taking great pains not to attract attention to herself, India nodded in the woman's direction, desperately trying to connect with the Guillemette she knew. But the woman was an empty shell. Through her eyes, she screamed at the woman, "I'm India, for God's sake, remember me. I can feed and hide you." For the briefest of moments, there was a spark of recognition in the woman's eyes. But with it came a clear reply;

Thank you. Bless you. My life is already dead; I will not compromise yours. And she walked on.

Over the years, there had been a few Believers who had taken shelter under her roof, many of them on their way to Italy where they were somewhat safer. Most stayed for only a few days, hidden away in the cellar where the fruits and vegetables were stored. They read to her from their good books and told her stories of seeing other Cathars living out meager existences in remote caves. But even they were not safe. They had been hunted down like wild animals and slaughtered, so India knew she was still among the hunted.

* * * *

As the hours passed, the noonday's heat weighed heavily on India's sleepy eyes. She struggled to stay awake, afraid of what the thin veils between then and now would recall. As her breathing relaxed and her head nodded forward in resignation, memories from the deepest shadows of her mind came streaming toward the light. Squeezing her eyes tight, she prayed God would not make her recall them, but it was of no use. She could remember it all—the clashes of steel, the screams of men plunging down sheer rocky slopes to their deaths, the thunder of battle, the rain on the courtyard stones, her own cries drowned by agonized echoes of others around her, the sky awash in a blood-red hue, and the weight of the secret she alone must bear.

A tear began to slide down her cheek, and she brushed it away with the impatience of a woman who had never been allowed the option of weakness.

The wooden floor was strewn with soiled straw that badly needed changing; the soured odor assaulted her nostrils, yanking her back to the present and irritating her even further in the process.

She knew she was dying, and although that should have brought her a sense of consolation, she was edgy and uncertain. It was too soon, and it was for this reason that she found herself sharp and impatient these days. She worried constantly. She had lived too long among these Christians, and she was tired. Too many things depended on her, and she fretted about the what-ifs. A promise hung by a thread and on a chance meeting.

Lately, she had contemplated writing down what she could before all was lost. In guarded words, she could at least leave enough clues to guide another to its location. Although it would be dangerous, she could not just sit day after day doing nothing. It was not in her nature to leave things to chance--or to God. The problem was that she might not have a choice, and she wrestled with this knowledge daily.

By now, Favia had returned and quickly set herself to completing her chores, attempting to look busy.

"What news, then, from the market?" India asked.

"None, Madame." Her response was barely sweet. "I spoke to no one as you instructed. Should I have?"

Cheeky bitch. "Get that clean straw down before it rains and tonight's meal prepared." She could feel in her bones that there was a storm coming.

Favia glanced outside at the sunshine, shrugged and continued on with her tasks.

Within hours, the sky grew dark and low rumblings rolled through the house as a thunderstorm threatened in the distance. Market stalls were being drawn up and vegetables and fruit carted away. Sharp-eyed, beggary children danced around, hoping for a stray bruised pear, amidst squawking chickens reluctantly flapping their way into burlap bags. Laborers and tenant farmers, who had toiled in the fields all day outside the city's protective walls, were trudging back home for the night, their bodies bent against the weight of their rakes and hoes. The air was heavy with dampness, and from the looks of it, tonight's storm promised to be severe.

* * * *

Later that night, India lay in her bed hardly daring to fall asleep. She must remember everything while she could. Yet another day was gone, bringing another night closer to death's door. The low rumblings of the storm outside issued a warning of what was to come, and she hoped he was not out on such a night as this. A sudden stab in her chest took her breath away, and she slowly breathed her way through the pain until it subsided.

Frightened, she felt she could wait no longer. It would be dangerous business committing what she knew to parchment, but she had no choice. Determined now, she rose slowly from her cot, lit a yellowed taper and by its dim glimmer began to write.

It is the year of our lord 1290 and having reached the end of my poor sinner's life, I, India Serras, now an old woman with only fading memories for company, choose to recall the events of my youth. It is a tale that even now, almost fifty years later, is still dangerous to speak of. Yet, for the sake of those who have gone before, and those who are yet to be born, the story must not die with me. My face and my body may have blended in with the others over the years, but my soul has remained true, for it is with heretic's eyes that I see, and a Cathar heart, soul and voice that I share my tale.

By my own account, I have been a liar, a thief and a murderess. I have loved a forbidden man, as passionately as any, and through circumstances not of my choice, I have become the keeper of a secret most grave. God, indeed, works in mysterious ways.

Committing words to paper could well be my undoing. It makes me a little giddy to do such a bold thing after so many years. I feel like I have awakened the daring girl inside of me for one last adventure, or perhaps ending. Who can say for certain? To whomever these words befall, you must listen very carefully, suspending all that you hold true, for I will never repeat these words again.

The thunder rolled deeply as the rain began to pelt down. Thick, heavy drops battered the old shutters with a promise that it would be a long, wet night. As she wrapped her shawl tighter, she shivered and tried to shake off a nagging feeling. Something did not bode well.

Chapter Two

Black as pitch it was, and the impotent flicker from Jourdain LeTardif's lantern had fizzled out hours ago; the incessant rain and chilling winds had seen to that. For two days he and Alfreid Boutarra, another merchant from Montaillou, had been traveling. Tonight their well-worn clothes were soaked and their hands frozen raw to the bone. Rain pelted their faces relentlessly, so their only recourse was to keep their heads low and entrust their weary horses to the muddy, sodden path.

Waves of thunder rumbled and rolled across the night sky until, in a deafening crescendo, it exploded and crackled its way into the darkness. In its wake, petulant fingers of lightning snatched menacingly at their heads as they plodded on. Since they had already traveled too far to stop, they trudged on, the lightening at least providing momentary confirmations as to their whereabouts.

"This is not a night for man nor beast!" Jourdain shouted over the rain. His temper was short, making it hard not to blame his wife Maura for their predicament. "But there's no time to stop until we've reached Carcassonne. Tomorrow the fair will begin and we must be there. Had I left when I wanted to we'd be in the city by now with the others, dry as a bone and warming ourselves by a hearth fire with a pint of good ale." Twisting his cloak a little tighter, he spat his frustration into the wind.

Alfreid looked up, squinting as the rain pelted his old face.

"C'est vrai, Jourdain. How different from last year, eh? We arrived days in advance, rose early and caught the best prices possible. Remember? You struck quite the bargain with that tanner from Cordova."

"Now, here we are behind a day's leaving," Jourdain grumbled, "riding through a thunderstorm because of a fearful woman's intuition and a long-winded priest."

Alfreid nodded. "It's no secret, Jourdain. Your Maura can interpret every manner of superstition between the sea and the far side of the mountains."

"Òc, and dole out a list of protective prayers just as long! We'll not likely find a room now; I'll tell you, the thought of spending the night in some dank moldy straw doesn't make me warm to the idea that at least my soul is safe from unnamed evils."

Rivulets of rain drizzled down from Jourdain's brow to the tip of his dripping nose, causing him to constantly wipe it with a cold, drenched sleeve. Shaking his head slowly, he let out a long slow sigh. He had held his tongue as he always did with Maura. What choice did he have?

She was a good woman and quick in the way of figures and managing a household, but she had a temper that meant business and lacked restraint. She truly believed that as long as she prayed fervently and believed totally, she could protect her family from evil. She had had such a bad feeling about this trip that she insisted their son, Leo, stay home. As if he could read his mind, Jourdain sheepishly glanced at Alfreid. It was no secret who made the decisions in his family.

They had attended her precious Mass, as she demanded. Although, Jourdain had mouthed the words, he felt divine communication was beyond the likes of a leather merchant. Never did he have, nor did he expect to have, direct communication with God. As he understood it, only priests intervened for the benefit of the unworthy masses. Maura had certainly drilled this into his head enough times. He was a sinner, an unworthy servant of a demanding, jealous God, and there would be no mercy for those who disobeyed Him, or His intermediaries for that matter.

Each Sunday was always the same. What did he really believe? Did Alfreid feel the same way? Was it even safe to ask? These days it was dangerous to question anything.

The road widened ahead, and Alfreid trotted up beside him.

"Are you sure Maura didn't pray for this weather to make you stay?"

Trust Alfreid to make him smile.

Steam rose from the nostrils of his exhausted mare as he prodded her to quicken her pace. His Sumter horse plodded along behind, snorting in resignation at the weight of his load. The muck of the road sucked at the horses' hooves slowing their progress. Jourdain pulled his cloak a little closer. Not that it did any good. His chest hurt, and his head ached so badly that he thought it would explode. The rain continued to beat down relentlessly, stinging his numbed cheeks and hands.

"That son of yours, Jourdain, is growing into a fine young lad. Leo might be helping you in your leather trade, but soon enough it'll be the other way around. How old is he now?"

"Fifteen this past spring. Set enough for the future if he works hard. He'll be joining me from now on, no matter what his mother says. Let the lad learn; that's what I say. He'll be taking the business over soon enough anyway. In not too many more years, he'll be taking a wife of his own."

"He's a big lad, your boy. But then, Maura's family is farm stock, isn't it? Time for another you think?"

"A daughter to help Maura around the house would be nice, but she was barely able to deliver Leo." Jourdain bowed his head lower. If prayers alone were enough, his home would be overrun with fat babies by now. Although she was able to conceive, three miscarriages over the last five years stood testament that there would likely be no more.

Suddenly the sky split apart, and a thunderclap blasted above their heads. His lead horse, already skittish, began to bolt as a heavy bough crashed somewhere close by.

"Arête, Othon, arête!" he yelled through the rain, his heart racing as he strained to control the frightened beast. With what strength he had left, he pulled at the soaked leather traces until his horse slowed to a trot and the others were forced to follow. Pitying the poor creature, Jourdain patted his slick steamy neck and was rewarded for his efforts with a bit of warmth as he stroked the tired mount. "It won't be long, old girl, not much longer now."

Turning to check the packhorse behind, he was relieved to see it was still in tow and his bags secure. The landscape, briefly illuminated, allowed them to see the city's towers ahead. Yes, just a little farther.

"With any luck, Alfreid, the city gates won't be shut for the night. I say we go through the nearest gate, the Cité, and head towards the inn. We'll make our way to the Ville Basse in the morning. To stay outside the city is to invite trouble. Thieves will be everywhere, and two lone merchants with full purses and goods are easy pickings. Keep your knife close."

"Ah, Jourdain, you are far too serious. Besides, there will be plenty of guards about. You worry like an old woman, or worse, like your wife. Now that we're near, can't you feel the excitement? We are here at Carcassonne during a fair! It is like a sleepy city that wakes up with a start, jumps out of bed, and cries, 'yes! I'm alive!' For two weeks, it has passion. Passion, Jourdain! And the women are beauties down to the last! Don't say you haven't noticed. A feast for the senses, that's what it is, mon ami; that is, indeed, what it is. It's a city alive with sounds of merchants and buyers bartering and making deals and pretty wenches offering their wares of flowers, vegetables, chickens, wine, beer, bread, and cakes. I can already taste the warm bread and some of that fine ale from the Widow Dumont. That woman has a gift, she does, and not just for her ale."

Jourdain chuckled to himself. Much to the chagrin of his wife, Alfreid always had a quick wink for any pretty lady. The inn would be full due to the fair, but after riding through that storm, some dry straw off in the corner by the hearth would suit them fine tonight. The warmth alone would be worth its weight in gold. Holding tightly onto the horse's traces, he noted the light of the cresset lamps that burned dimly in the distant windows. They were in luck, but since Jourdain did not want to take any chances, they entered the Cite, the first gate available.

The pungent familiar odor of the city assaulted their nostrils, and the clip clop of their horses' hooves now on the cobblestones of the narrow dank lane made the next twenty minutes feel like forever. The rain had dwindled in intensity but was still creating a symphony of sound as waterfalls cascaded from the rooftops and splashed into puddles on the cobblestones below. Filth and raw sewage floated down shallow ditches, while a scrawny yellow dog relieved itself. Bodies huddled close together in doorways with silent eyes that watched them from everywhere. It had been foolish of them to have taken this chance and traveled through the night.

"Keep your eyes about you, Alfreid. Judging from the rank odor, we're near the Tanners, which means we're several streets north of where we need to be. This would not be a good night to be lost, my friend."

Alfreid responded with a sleepy nod. "You lead, I'll follow. Just wake me when we get to the inn."

Tired, chilled and mentally sorting out his directions, Jourdain didn't notice the ragged young man until he was upon him.

"Alfreid, thieves!" Jourdain's hand moved quickly to the small blade by his side. He looked around, expecting to be accosted by more men, but was momentarily relieved that there was only one. His body tense, he prepared to shove the young lad off or fight if he needed to. In that moment of hesitation, however, he glimpsed two larger, quicker shadows and a flash of steel before feeling a searing pain in his arm.

The next few moments were only a blur. Rough hands grabbed at his cloak and attempted to pull him out of his saddle. Alfreid gave a deep-throated yell of pain as his bloodied hands grasped at his neck. Jourdain frantically turned his horse to block their attempts and trample them if he could, but the streets were narrow and the horses panicked. From the corner of his eye, he saw Alfreid fall, and turned to look. There on the blood-soaked cobblestones lay his old friend, eyes bulging, staring towards Jourdain in a moment of disbelief as he gurgled his last breaths.

Jourdain snapped. His heart pumping, adrenalin rushing through his veins, he roughly booted his horse's flanks hoping to at least escape with his life. A second villain had already cut loose the pack horses, and as another tried again to pull him off his mount, he booted his assailant a mighty blow to his head, pushing him backwards on to the street. In an instant, he took off, only vaguely aware of a darkening stain on his sleeve and a pain in his side. Alfreid was dead. He had lost everything. Not knowing or caring where he was headed, he urged his horse on into the blackness of the city streets.

* * * *

When the tumultuous storm had passed, it left in its wake a hollow echo of silence through the city's narrow streets. The air was heavy and damp with the night's precipitation, and a thick mist began winding through the city streets like a long, stealthy snake. The fog engulfed the shadows and veiled the rooftops and tattered shutters with a moist patina of dulled silver. At such a late hour, the city gave the appearance of being dead, but through the mist, a single spectral light flickered through the slats of an upper story window.

Doubled over and tightly clutching his horse's traces to keep from falling, Jourdain was frantically searching for safety when his eye caught the light. He suddenly felt a surge of hope and aimed his horse toward the lone candle. He would not die in these streets this night, that he vowed. With his last bit of energy, he slid gingerly from his horse and pounded heavily on the door of the building. Unable to stand any longer, and barely conscious, he collapsed in a heap at the doorstep. As the city slept, a rat scuttled across his foot in the darkness. He shivered his revulsion and the world went black.

Chapter Three

Old oaken beams reluctantly creaked their way open as Favia peered through a crack in the darkness. She started to immediately shut the door, but her attempt was interrupted by India's walking cane wedged in from behind.

"What's going on?"

"Nothing, Madame, just an old drunk at our doorstep. He'll be gone by morning."

India pushed aside her servant to have a look. From the flickering yellow light of her candle, she could see the lump of a man's figure laying crumpled on the doorstep. She needed no confirmation as to his condition. His blood-soaked body said it all.

"Where's your mind, girl? He's not drunk; he's been injured. We need to get him out of this damp and inside by the fire."

"By the look of it, I'll need some hot water and plenty of it. Get the neighbor's stable boy, Pierre, to help you get him inside. Stoke the fire, fetch a warm blanket and then get the boy to tend to this man's horse. I'll tend to his wounds myself."

From Favia's pout, it was obvious she had already sized up her own situation. The stranger was trouble and meant extra work.

"Don't stand there with your mouth open. Be quick about it, lazy child." India held her taper closer to have a better look at the stranger's wounds and the quality of man at her doorstep. He seemed to be about forty years of age, with a pleasant face that sparked no feeling of danger within her. His worn, old clothing was soaked through, but it had good workmanship, nonetheless, and his horse was clearly exhausted. He was most likely a merchant in town for the fair and just another victim of

25

local thieves. But still, she sensed there was something unusual about this man that she could not name or put into words. He had obviously lost much blood, and he winced when she examined the wound. She thought of a small herbal mixture that worked well with this type of injury and strained her memory to remember the combination.

"What's taking that girl so long?"

Momentarily conscious, the stranger's eyes fluttered, and he attempted to speak. She instantly shushed him into silence. There would be plenty of time for talking later, if he lived.

* * * *

Jourdain's first sense of consciousness was of immense pain that enveloped his entire being. His throat was swollen, and it hurt to swallow. His voice seemed distant and hoarse. He was vaguely aware of someone placing a hot, wet cloth on his throat, and the room reeked with some kind of vile-smelling ointment. There was a hot stone at his feet, and when he tried to lift his right arm, he could not. Overcome with weakness and nausea, he closed his eyes and fell into another deep sleep. He drifted in and out of consciousness, not entirely aware of where he was. He was only vaguely aware of hot liquid being occasionally put to his lips.

He awoke next to a profound weakness and numbness in his entire body. There was a milky film over his vision, which made it difficult to see. The air was warm, and the room was filled with fetid and dusty odors, and the cries of a marketplace that seeped through the plastered walls. A young girl was sitting by his bed, cupping one hand under a spoon and encouraging him to sip the broth. The smell awakened pangs of hunger, and he responded weakly. The bit of nourishment was good, and a little strength surged into his body. He tried to say thank you, but his voice still seemed distant. The girl curled her lips into a vague smile that held no warmth. She merely looked at him with her hollow eyes, got up and left.

Days blended into nights until he was no longer sure which was which. He was vaguely aware of being watched. Sometimes he could discern the sound of light breathing coming from the corner of the room. At other times, he could feel the merest hint of a breeze or swish from a skirt as his observer, just barely out of his sight, escaped detection.

The smell of bread caused his stomach to growl, and the muffled sounds of market day reminded him of why he was there. Each day the young girl came to wordlessly feed him broth and help him to relieve himself. Each day he grew a little stronger. He spent hours piecing together flashes of what he remembered from his foggy memory--the rain, thieves and Alfreid. His heart was heavy at the last memory of his friend. Where was he? How long had he been here? What had he lost? He lay there for a few moments trying to recall all that had happened, surely only just the night before, but the details were still fuzzy and misplaced.

"Where am I?" he whispered aloud. The last thing he expected was a reply.

"My name, Monsieur, is India Serras, and you are a guest in my home." The voice was that of an old woman and seemed to come from the dark corner to his right. "You have met with some misfortune, and fate has found you a safe bed for the past fortnight. I am most pleased that your health is progressing well enough for us to chat."

His hostess stepped out of the shadows, and in the candle's thin, wavering flicker he caught his first glimpse of the person who was speaking. Before him stood an ancient willow of a woman. Withered and bent, wrapped in an old woolen shawl too large for her diminutive frame, she reminded him of a child in her mother's clothes. Indeed, her garments hung so loosely that they looked as if either they were not her own, or her body had been greatly altered through the years. She leaned on an old, carved wooden cane that caught his eye immediately because it's obvious cost and workmanship was completely opposite from its ragged owner. Exquisitely carved with circlets and a fine silvered cap at the base, it was certainly one of the most beautiful walking canes he had ever seen. There was obviously more to this woman than what met the eye.

"You are feeling better these days." This was not a question, but a statement. She tripped a little as she shuffled closer and leaned heavily on her cane to regain her balance.

Jourdain tried to sit up, the better to assess his situation, but she shushed him back down with the iron will of a woman who was used to being obeyed. He complied surprised that such a confident command should come from such a minute lady.

"A fortnight has gone by, then," he said, wincing at the implications. Alfreid was surely dead. He had missed the fair and lost everything. Financially, his family would barely make it through the winter months. With a deep sigh, he also realized this woman had saved his life. "I am in deepest gratitude to you, dear lady. Without your expert care I would have surely died. You are obviously skilled in the healing arts."

She drew close and smiled. "More than you know."

As he looked up, he caught his breath, as the intensity of her gaze seemed to draw him near. Her eyes were an intense blue that belied her wispy ancient frame. These were the eyes of strength, youth and courage. He felt strangely that, somehow, their meeting was no accident. Indeed, it was as if she had demanded his presence; he, having no choice in the matter, had come.

"Madame," he replied weakly, "I do not know what I have, but as God is my word, I will repay your kindness." His head began to hurt, and an overwhelming fatigue overcame him.

"Hush!" she barked. "There will be no talk of payment between us."

Unraveling the bandages from around his arm, India examined the wound. It had been deep, but thankfully it had missed any major arteries. It was clean, and she bound it back tightly. A tiny breeze teased a wisp of her snow-white hair as she absent-mindedly patted it into place. She was intent upon her guest.

Beads of sweat dotted his upper lip, and she worried that the fever had returned. She'd have to watch him closely. Was it a coincidence that this stranger appeared the very night she chose to write what she should not? Who was he? Certainly it was not who she expected and yet--there was something familiar about him, something that tugged at her memory.

"Keep your coins, for what do I care for money at my age?" She turned to walk away, somewhat offended, but then stopped and slowly faced her guest.

There was an awkward moment of silence pregnant with an unnamed request. The stranger before her taunted her with possibilities. She had always assumed that he would have been a Templar, or that at least he would openly declare himself. She chastised herself for being an old fool, but she still needed a sign to let her know that her tale would fall on safe ears. She prayed for something that might help her see that he was, indeed, who she so desperately needed him to be.

"Monsieur, how is it that you are called?"

"Jourdain LeTardif, Madame. I am a leather merchant from Montaillou." At the mention of his name, she was visibly shaken but regained herself. She had not heard that name in years.

"You must rest," she commanded, for he was still very weak.

His eyes closed, and she waited until he easily fell into a deep sleep.

Her hands trembling, she gently pulled down the blankets a little to reveal what she already knew she would find. On the back of his left shoulder blade was the red cross-patois birthmark. Shaken, she realized with absolute certainty who the sleeping man was.

"Although you do not know me, Monsieur, our lives are intertwined." She spoke her words softly, but purposely. "I have been waiting for you, for longer than you know."

There were no doubts. There was no more time, and she knew it. There was no other choice but to write her thoughts, her fears and the truth of what happened now, for she wouldn't last the month. The pains in her chest were sharper these days, and her breathing labored and difficult. She had only two priorities left, and they were to finish her journals and ensure that this man lived. Everything must be written down, and all her secrets revealed.

She shifted herself, in order to directly face her sleeping patient, and whispered, "I barely hoped that I would be fortunate enough to see you even once more before I died. We have much to talk about, you and I. Sleep well, for there is much that you need to know."

Gathering her wits about her, she started to leave, but then she became anxious about how to begin and what to say that would not frighten him away. "Look at him," she whispered. "He's not a boy. He's a grown man and the very image of his father."

Chapter Four

Mémoires de India Serras

I write now with wisdom that I should have had when I was far younger. I have found that wisdom is wasted on the old. The young don't want to hear it, and by the time you're blessed with enough of it, you're far too old to appreciate it. But write I must, with honestly and truth, for I have nothing left to lose and everything to gain. False statements are forbidden in my faith, and although I have intentionally deceived many over the years, I do not lie now when I write my words.

I hardly know where to begin, for there is so much that needs to be told. Some things I remember well, as if it were yesterday, but others are like searching through a fog. I am afraid that one day I will forget everything. Some days I think it might not be such a bad idea. The very best I can do is to beg you to indulge the writings of an old woman until my tale is told in full. I can only trust that you will read my story in confidence for not until I am through will you understand the full gravity of my words.

I am old now, too old for things of the heart, things of this earth. I can only pray that God will be kind and soon allow me to join those I love, even though my body has been unclean these many years. I have eaten meat, committed grave sins and told lies. I have renounced my own, and in so doing, I betrayed those whom I loved most. I have seen those I love purified in the heretic's fire, and I do not wish these memories on anyone. I had a child. I know that because of my earthly needs my soul may not be released; I can only pray that by completing what has been asked of me, all will be forgiven. At least that is what has been promised to me.

At night, before I retire, I allow myself the little rituals of my faith. Under my shift, I still wear my Perfect's cord. Dangerous I know, but a delicious little secret I allow myself these days. I take out the ring from my love, Durand, given to me by him so long ago, and as always, I wonder about him and our son. After so many years, I imagine my own version of events, one where those I loved did not die but where we had years together.

At least for tonight, I am my true self while I sit and scratch my words. Everything else about me is just a lie. By day, I am just an old woman of no consequence or use except to employ those to do what I can no longer do myself. False documents have me known as a widow. This much is true, although, were I to name my true beloved they would not hesitate to call me unflattering names. Such is life.

I think the only time I feel safe is late at night in my room. I have reasoned over the years that if they were to come for me, it would be during the daylight hours. In my mind at day's end, I always feel like I have cheated the Inquisition until the next first light. Now, after so many years, I suspect that it will be my old age and a failing heart that will cause my demise and take with it a secret yet untold.

My father told me once that when I was born, he looked into my eyes and saw the warrior that my soul had been before, and he was frightened by my strength. Perhaps my mother, knowing that she would not survive the month, gave what was left of hers to me. I like to think that, and for this reason, I suppose I always knew what my future would hold.

Many of us thought that it would all eventually stop, and all would be well. The French would wait it out; we would plant more crops to replace savaged fields, rebuild and reunite. No one could guess just how black our future would become. But then, I am ahead of my tale. I should, I suppose, begin where my life truly began.

It must be stated here that I did not start out jaded and worn. In truth, I was an inquisitive child, and oddly enough considering my situation, full of hope and dreams of love as all young girls are. In that respect, I was no different from any other girl. I had my household duties to tend to~mending, cleaning, minding the accounts, all manner of tedious chores~but I also had a penchant for swordplay. I actually wrote to my father and informed him that I had decided not to be a girl. I wanted to become a boy and should be provided the education more suited to my new sex.

You may smile, but I tell you it was so. I imagined myself quite the lady knight, riding on ahead of a brave band of routiers, my red hair flying in the wind like an emblazoned banner. I was glorious, bold and victory was mine. Never in those childhood dreams did I imagine that this would be so close to the truth. When I was a little girl of six, I begged my father for a tutor to teach me to handle a sword, but he refused. This was not the Cathar way.

When I was twelve, we traveled to visit relatives of my mother's, and it was here that I heard first-hand of the dark rumors. It was not a long journey, only two days by horseback, but my father and I rode with a small group of merchants for safety's sake.

I remember every step of that journey. Snow still blanketed the peaks, and the cool crisp air was a refreshing change from the smoke-filled rooms of our house.

When we finally arrived at my uncle's, it was late in the evening and a warm meal awaited us. My three little cousins had grown much since our last visit, and I hardly recognized them. Cecile was my around my age and had just celebrated her thirteenth year that past month. Jeannette was ten and Marie-Clare, six. My aunt made a great fuss over how much I resembled my mother, and I remember feeling very pleased about that. My cousins and I slept in the loft in one great bed, and it was there that I first realized the depth of the persecutions.

When we finally got the two youngest to sleep, Cecile whispered to me that she had heard some frightening news. Slipping out of bed, we wrapped ourselves in a blanket and crept over to where the ladder met the loft and we could listen to our parents. My uncle was telling my father that he was very worried about the future. The Roman church was becoming very powerful and obsessed with eradicating its perceived enemies. It was no secret to anyone that the Christian's clergy were living off the sweat of its followers. These "holy" men were shams, and many of them lived lustful, materialistic lives.

As we listened, Cecile and I hugged each other tight. Northern French Barons and the Church were creating many problems for anyone of the Cathar faith. Everyone agreed that the church wouldn't dare harm anyone. The entire region of Òc was Cathar, and we hadn't done anything. We Believers were quiet people and didn't carry our religion in our pockets. Our communities were prosperous and cooperative. But we were in direct opposition to what the Orthodox Catholics taught because we insisted on direct and personal knowledge. We did not believe in the need for an ordained intermediary between man and God. We knew that love and power were incompatible as had been proven many times by the Catholic clerics themselves.

Cecile and I crept back to our bed, and with an ominous feeling, fell into a deep sleep. We stayed for two months, and although we had many times filled with laughter, the sight of my father and uncle talking well into the night, and to the rest of the community, was enough to bring my feelings of foreboding back with a resounding jolt. We were taught to not fear death, but I can tell you we were terrified.

As we left, I took one long, last look at the craggy mountain village. That is my last memory of my cousins, for I would never see them again. The crusaders' army attacked Moisseau the following year. After the town was sacked, homes burned and women and young girls raped, one hundred and ninety men, women and children were massacred. My uncle, my aunt and my three young cousins were among them.

It was this incident, more than any other that would determine the path I would take, for I was never the same. I was not like the others. I couldn't sit by and pretend that everything would return to normal. I believed the madness would never end, no matter what we did or what we believed. This was indeed hell on earth. Fire burned in my heart, and the sparks ignited flaming the coals of anger. My innocence died that day. I buried it alongside my cousins and then whispered a goodbye to their spirits. This is the moment when my warrior-self came forth from the shadows of my soul. It was the moment when I knew my destiny. I would fight and I would kill. What I could not have predicted, was the hell that was yet to come.

Kate Riley

Chapter Five

Renier de Beynac drummed a tattoo on the table's edge while he compulsively searched for any signs of dirt on the other. Finally, noting a small smear on his lower right palm, he delicately pulled out an embroidered handkerchief from his left sleeve and religiously scrubbed it clean. This discovery provoked further scrutinizing in case he had missed a spot on either hand. Leaning back in his leather chaise, he primly crossed his legs and gave his hands one last glance. Although he couldn't stand them being dirty, that wasn't what was really irritating him.

His lips were pursed, tightened into a thin line, in an effort to regain control of his anger, for he had just received two letters of correspondence. One lay open proudly on his desk, while the other had been crumbled and tossed angrily to the floor missing the hearth fire by mere inches.

The letter on the desk was a commendation from his Holiness Innocent III for a task delicately stated as "well executed." He actually had smiled at the phrasing when he first read it. One could read so much in a word. The second was from a legal cleric who wrote on behalf of his older brother Eduarde. The letter was simply factual, stating that Eduarde, eldest son of the Knight Etienne de Beynac, grandson of the esteemed and honorable Knight, Jean de Beynac, was ill and would not likely survive the summer. Upon the event of his death, due to lack of any progeny, Renier would inherit whatever was left of what Eduarde had not drunk or gambled away. His brother had hoped that Renier would return home in order to repair their familial bonds. All this really meant was he wanted to ensure his own soul's eternal salvation. Let him rot in hell.

As far as Renier was concerned, there was no love between him and his brother, so there was no sense of urgency to sit by his deathbed and listen to regrets. So long. Bonjour. The impudence of Eduarde's attempt for a deathbed apology brought too many bitter memories along with it, and he struggled to keep them at bay.

He eyed the commendation from the Pope with some frustration. He was a well-respected member of the inquisition, and his father should have been pleased, indeed proud, of Renier and his accomplishments. It was largely due to his personal efforts, after all, that the majority of Cathar stragglers were even found. If one were to really think about it, his father should have been proud of him thousands of times over, but nothing he did was ever good enough to merit so much as a nod in his direction. The bastard even had the audacity to die before Renier had a chance to rub it in his face. He slumped farther into his chair, took a large gulp of wine from a silver goblet and kicked the letter into the fire. And then there was Eduarde. As the edges singed and burned, he stared into the flames, unconsciously shifting his thoughts to childhood memories that had been bottled up for far too long.

As the youngest son, with seven years between him and his brother, Renier had neither illusion of titles nor wealth. It was always known that Eduarde would inherit the lion's share of his father's meager estates, while he must make his way by cleric or clergy. He had hoped, though, that he would inherit something that would indicate he was of value. The three most influential men in his life--his grandfather, father and brother--had always shunned him. The physical difference between him and his beefy, older brother was a constant source of debate, and they made no secret of doubting his parentage. The thought of them brought tightness to his face and bile to his stomach. Unable now to stop the memories, they flooded and churned their way to the surface He endured the scenes playing out before him as they always had since the age of ten.

He could hear his father drinking and boasting to the other men that his eldest son, Eduarde, was a man of whom anyone could be proud. Eduarde was strong. Eduarde was comely. Eduarde was clever, not like his scrawny, youngest whelp, Renier, sniveling in the corner. He should have left him at home with the other girls.

"If I could have drowned him at birth with a sack of pups I would have, for I knew he'd be good for nothing but draining my hard-earned resources and his brother's legacy. Look at the thin pathetic thing he is. He's not from my loins, that one."

If his father had been drinking enough, it was his mother who would then receive the back of his hand and a beating for the betrayal of burdening him with such a son. Even though she vehemently denied any betrayal to her dying breath, Renier also grew to hate her. It was obvious that had the bitch kept to her husband's bed he would be a younger version of Eduarde: stronger, smarter, a man worthy of his father's love.

Now unleashed, other memories came floating back. They were loaded with beatings and abuse, not just from his father, but from his brother as well. He could still see the cynical glaze in his father's eyes as Renier was repeatedly beaten, slapped or kicked--simply because he was in the wrong place at the wrong time, because he was weak, or because he was simply alive. Then there was Eduarde's even darker secret.

His brother, ever the apple of his father's eye, had his own form of torture that he exercised when his prey was alone, weak and vulnerable. It was one that Renier endured in shamed silence in darkened corners and livestock byres. It was of little consolation that years later it was he, and not his drunken lout of a brother, who attained Papal esteem. It was he who had money, and he who would have deserved his father's pride, not that bastard.

Nothing he ever did warranted a smile or a pat on the head from that man. Nothing that he said was even the slightest bit worthwhile. Instead, his father was embarrassed at the sight of him, never failing to tell him he lacked a backbone, a man's drive, a man's strength, a man's cock.

The kidney pie he had eaten at dinner rose uncomfortably in his stomach. The more agitated he became, the more the bile built up. The urges hit again. The tension always made him anxious, nervous, and stiffened his member with sexual feelings he couldn't stop.

Suddenly, he was ten and memories flooded back--the beatings, the unspeakable things, the splitting pain from behind and his brother's sneering laughter. Always the laughter. He could still hear the grunting, the final groan, the way his brother always wiped himself all over Renier's bare ass. He remembered the tears, the anger, the shame until

37

the next time, and the next, and the next, until he started to like it, need it, crave it. It was then that it ended, forcing him to satisfy himself, developing his own taste for other's pain. That was what really aroused his senses and the younger the better. He had tried whores and older women, but the act was always perfunctory, simply an outlet for tension. The real enticement was pain and the control over another's life. The ultimate moment of power made him want more.

He had loved a girl once when he was fifteen. She was his age, lovely and feral. The daughter of the cook, she had long, curly, jet black hair and dark, endless eyes. Her breasts swelled as if they were about to burst through the top of her bodice making his cock stiffen every time he saw. He wanted her like he had never wanted anyone or anything in his life, and he dreamt of her wanting him to spill his seed in her nightly.

Soon every glance was confirmation that she felt the same way. She knew, the bitch. She knew the power she had over him, as she enticed him with smiles and those milky white breasts with dark brown nipples that demanded his mouth, his hands, his tongue. What happened next was her own damned fault.

When he could stand it no longer, he waited and cornered her one day in the barn, spewing sweet words while he fumbled and groped at those ripe apples of hers. But what did he get for that pleasure? A slap and shrill uncontrollable laughter. Shocked, he took a step back, let go of her and held his cheek.

"What's so funny?" he demanded.

"You are. Your words are. Your intentions are. Everyone knows that you're nothing but a milksop, your brother's little barnyard 'pet'. You're physically incapable of being with a woman." She laughed and kept on laughing. "Just wait until everyone hears this one. Run along, little pet, so I can find a real man to satisfy me."

Blinded by rage and anger, he snapped. Grabbing her bodice, he ripped downward so that her breasts were completely exposed, nearly driving him to insanity. Shocked, she attempted to run away, but he was quicker. Roughly throwing her to the ground in a frenzy of sexual excitement, he took control. For the first time in his life, he could do whatever he wanted. She fought like a she-wolf, biting, scratching and hitting him, but this only encouraged him, making him stronger. He bit back, pinned her arms and suckled hard, bruising, tearing whatever he could until her thighs were exposed, her body bare and ready. He was harder than he had ever been and aroused beyond belief. He thrust himself upon her and entered her roughly, savagely, pounding until he released all his anger into one intense moment of ecstasy. Then, when it was over, and she lay whimpering, he wiped himself on her belly, calmly stood up, grabbed the pitchfork and hit her again and again. Ravaged, her throat severed, her face slashed, one eye dangling from its socket, she lay dead in the bloodied hay. He smiled at the memory of his first love and the look of horror and fear on the faces of his father and brother when they discovered what he had done. In that moment, he understood where his power lay and exactly how to use it.

"Well, who has the backbone now, Eduarde? Who does His Holiness admire? Who is invited to the best courts, the best parties? It is me, Eduarde. Why, just yesterday my presence was requested at the Cardinal's court in Carcassonne. I have everything a civilized man could want. I have books to read, coins for my purse, expensive silk hose, furs, whores and other playthings anytime I please. I have made a fine income accepting bribes and fines from the wealthy who paid to avoid being prosecuted. I have respect from my peers, and my name instills fear. You mean nothing to me Eduarde. May you burn in hell," he sneered.

Frustrated now, he brushed off an urge to release himself sexually and considered the offer from the Cardinal. He didn't like the man, and in all likelihood, the request was motivated by his recent paean from His Holiness, but no matter. He had already made quite a mess with a young urchin he had picked up last week and was concerned lest his appetite for the macabre be discovered. Provincial courts could be so tedious, but perhaps Carcassonne might be a diversion. He needed to get his mind off things. He was too tense, and he always knew where that led.

Chapter Six

India awakened early the next morning, feeling more eager to meet the day than she had in years. Still, she knew she must be careful not to get too excited, not to make her heart beat so fast that the dizzy spells became worse. She paced herself through her morning ablutions. There was so much to say and so little time in which to say it. She smiled to herself. How ironic it was that after so many years of waiting, what she so desperately needed right now was more time.

Making her way down the narrow hallway, she lightly touched cane to floor as quietly as she could. Taking small, slow steps, she reached the end of his bed, calmed her breathing and smiled. He was still asleep.

It was unfortunate that a knife wound had brought him to her, but what else but a bad wound would have made him stay? How incredible it was to have him here at all. God, indeed, worked in wondrous ways. India couldn't stop looking at him. She felt like a mother gazing at her newborn babe--feelings she had not experienced in years. She watched him like this for some time until Jourdain stirred and slowly opened his eyes. Seeing her there, he shifted his weight and winced in his attempt to turn a little too quickly.

"Madame ..."

"No. Don't get up, Jourdain, rest. I see your strength has increased a little. This is very good indeed, but you need to stay where you are."

"Thank you. I guess I am still a little unsure of myself."

"Perhaps by the end of the week you'll be ready to exercise your lower limbs, but for now, this is best," she said smiling. "Besides, if you fall, an old woman like me will be of no use in getting you back up again. How's the pain today? Better or the same?"

"A bit better, I think."

"Good. I'll warrant your fever has broken as well. Did Favia offer you something to eat?"

"I confess, Madame, she has not, but perhaps she saw me to be asleep and was busy with her chores. I don't want to be any trouble. I am happy to wait."

India stamped her cane on the dusty floorboards. "Forgive me, Monsieur, but I am an old woman, and she sorely taxes my patience. What little I have left, anyway." She tapped her cane even louder to attract her servant's attention from the floor below. "Favia, Favia, bring our guest some refreshment and something solid to eat, and be quick about it." She nodded to Jourdain. "I know, well, she's downstairs either eavesdropping or daydreaming about some market-boy 'prince.' Besides, it'll do you some good to get some nourishment."

From the floor below, Favia's muted response was a dull but swift thud with her broom to the ceiling. "Right away, Madame."

India cocked her ear to ensure that her servant was actively following her orders. When satisfied, she turned her attention once again to her patient. "See? I told you. My eyesight may be failing me, but there's nothing wrong with my old ears. I wish you would have known me when I was younger."

Making her way slowly to her chair by the fire, she lamented, "Look at me. My skin has become wrinkled and withered. My curves have melted into flab, like lard on a hot summer's day. So very flattering. But these are things of the flesh and really no longer matter."

At last, reaching her destination, she settled herself into a sturdy wooden chair. Lost within herself, she absent-mindedly adjusted a coverlet. "There are times when I do not feel this aged body nor my many, many years. When I close my eyes, it is easy for me to think that I am a younger version of myself; but when I open my eyes, it is my hands that rudely awaken me, reminding me that I am truly just an aged old woman."

She lifted her hands to her eyes and slowly turned them around. "Would you believe these hands have wielded a sword and healed the best of men? What a pity there is nothing to show their past valor. How brave and strong they were. These humble hands have held sacred things and calmed dying men's hearts, and now there's only a bitter old woman to really see them as they were. Can you guess that I am seventy-one years old today?"

"Seventy-one, Madame? Why that is quite an exceptional accomplishment, indeed."

"An accomplishment? Ha! I suppose that's one way to think of it. I am now even older than the Pope, if you can imagine that. Has it come to this, that even I must gauge my longevity by his Holiness on high? In my many years, I have seen a multitude of them come and go. Yet one thing has remained the same for each--their lusty greed for money has far exceeded any lofty goals towards spiritual enlightenment." She quickly stole a glance at Jourdain to gauge his reaction and caught the corner of a smile.

The smile was all the encouragement she needed to carry on.

"Why, I hear that our latest Papal appointee, a cobbler's son, has taken up the family business of selling forgiveness. Ah well, for those with a fine purse all manner of crimes can be forgiven. From murder to rape, no sin is too large that salvation cannot be bought by this Papa Domini." She straightened her shawl and brushed off a crumb. "I know I'm rambling on, but his followers are welcome to their ambitious lords, their bloody crusades, their Italian wars and their insatiable greed. My consolation is that I am not long for this world. Are you uncomfortable, sir? Or, perhaps you think these to be the ramblings of a crazy old woman?"

"No, not at all, although I am at a loss for words. I am quite sure you are aware that to openly question faith is to place yourself in a precarious position. We are supposed to just accept that we are on the right side, God's side, and follow what we are told to do. I confess that has always bothered me. How does anyone know for sure who is right? With my own eyes, I have seen a fear-induced husband disavow his wife to the black Dominicans. I have often questioned if this can truly be an expression of God's love."

Their attention was suddenly turned toward Favia stomping up the stairs.

Jourdain eyed the doorway. "Forgive me, Madame, but in these days of ignorance and superstition no one is to be trusted, no one."

India turned her head towards the door and fell silent. He was right, of course. How silly of her. She was excited, but conversations like this required the right ears for safety's sake.

Favia noisily clogged her way into the room carrying two pints of temperate ale and a loaf of seed cake on a wooden tray. Depositing her load on a small trestle table beside the bed, she turned with hands on hips, and faced India." I presume, Madame, that I am now allowed to go to the market and continue my chores?"

India glanced over at Jourdain, then back to Favia. It was all she could do to not scold the chit's attitude, but time alone with Jourdain was far more important. Instead, she replied with a strained smile, "Bien sur. Off you go, and if you don't forget those herbs I asked for, there will be no need to hurry back."

Favia snapped a quick look at India, obviously not expecting her sweet tone. "I'll be off then. Merci, Madame."

India smiled to Jourdain as Favia practically flew down the stairs and out the door.

"Forgive me. I don't get many visitors, and I forget that these are still dangerous times. People are an ignorant, bigoted and superstitious lot so easily appeased by blood and so easily intimidated by fear. Only my memories keep me company now. Some whisper to me in the dark, surrounding me like a worn old blanket keeping me warm. Others cut me deeply, and my heart bleeds. I was never cut out to be a helpless old woman." She slowly leaned forward and addressed him intently. "I shall speak honestly to you, Jourdain, for at long last the truth will cost me nothing. After so long, the freedom to do so is sweet bliss. To finally sit with you and tell my tale makes every moment worthwhile. I cannot truthfully remember a time when I have not feared for my life. To be known even now would cost me a heretic's fire to be sure."

"Madame!" Jourdain's hand flew up in panic. "I beg you stop! Say no more! If anything, his Holiness' lust for monies and women is common talk, but only a heretic, an enemy of the true church, would be threatened by the stake. Please, I am most grateful for your kindness and care, but if you are what I now suspect you to be, I would be guilty by association. Ultimately, I would be placing my family under suspicion as well. I confess that I have questions and doubts, but I am no heretic."

43

"Jourdain," she continued, "this aged woman before you is old and tired. Each night I hope for redemption from this physical body, but it seems that each morning I awaken to yet another day. Surely, you must wonder why I speak so freely to you and declare myself to be Cathar. Yes, I said, Cathar. I will not use the term heretic for that is a Christian's definition of who I am, not mine."

The look on his face confirmed his fear. He might turn her in, or worse, leave, but her words were loosened, and there would be no stopping her.

"I used to believe that those of my faith were cowards who would not fight but instead go willingly to their deaths. I was angry then, angry at so many things–at burnt bodies, my father for not protecting me and Durand for dying. I was angry at the world for leaving me alone." She stared hard. "I did not even have my child to keep me company. In my silent world, I screamed to be heard, to touch someone familiar. Through all these years no one has come, and I had almost given up hope, until now."

She could see he was dumbfounded, shocked into silence. This was her moment of opportunity. It was now or never; she had already said too much.

"Shall we see of what quality and manner of man you are, sir? If you are so intent on repaying me, I will place a proposition squarely on your lap for I have little time left for games and idle talk. Should you choose to accept, I will make you a rich man. Your life will never be the same again. Should you choose to decline, you will owe me nothing for my kindness, except your silence."

"However, I must first extract a pledge that what I have already said to you today must go no farther than this room. To do so would place both of us on the inquisition's burning pyres, and you are quite right that to damn yourself to such an end would also damn your family. My request is simple. Hold your judgment for just a little while longer and listen to the ramblings of an old woman. Not only will I make you a wealthy man, the tale may also touch your heart. You see, Jourdain Le Tardif from Montaillou, I know who you are and you do not!"

* * * *

Jourdain's heart pounded. She was right. If he went to the authorities, it would only place himself and his family under suspicion. No one was safe from the Dominicans' eyes, and he was already implicated by being in her home.

He sat in stunned silence not knowing what to say. Perhaps she was insane and thought him to be someone else. He weighed his options. She had saved his life and wanted him to listen to a story. In return, she would pay him well. This would repay the money and goods he had lost through the thieves. Glancing at her fine cane, he suspected money, perhaps even heirlooms, had been secretly buried somewhere. Undoubtedly, she was now too old to retrieve it herself. It was common knowledge that many Cathar families had hidden their treasures to escape plundering and losing them forever. He had no doubts as to what Maura would advise him to do, but India's words rang through his head. *"I know who you are and you do not,"* and they stirred emptiness inside him.

Returning her strong gaze, he slowly nodded in numbed agreement. There, it was done, and perhaps himself as well.

She smiled and looked deeply into his eyes. "It is agreed then."

They sat in silence for a few minutes, neither saying a word. No doubt, she was digesting what they had just agreed to, just as he was. How would this change his life? Only time would tell.

Chapter Seven

Renier had decided to wait until the Hot Fair was over by at least a week before traveling to Carcassonne. With the current heat, the stench would be unbearable. Besides, excellent bargains could now be had from merchants more than eager to sell. This made much more sense, for too many unwashed peasants overwhelmed his delicate sense of smell.

He blessed his foresight in having brought extra lavender sachets as he maneuvered on foot through the busy market streets. Noisy taverns, filled to the brim with tradesmen and merchants swilling back beer, spilled their drunken customers out into the streets. From tightly packed stalls, hawkers sold peacocks, thrushes and hares. There were nightingales in cages, baskets and wares of every description, bales of finest wool, ells of cloth in every hue and color, spices heaped in pyramids and fish swimming in leather pots smeared with resin and pitch. The merchants, identifying him by his clothes as a man with means, and therefore coin, spread their wares out, broadened their smiles and shouted to attract his attention and tempt him closer. Pretty girls in yellow hoods, whose breasts were enticingly exposed, smiled promises of heavenly delights should he choose their company. He smiled back. Perhaps later, should he not find a little something more to his liking.

Brushing his way through the crowds, he stopped to watch a troupe of jongleurs with a dancing bear that had a small group of children enthralled. The huge beast, dressed in a peaked cap and embroidered vest, towered above his trainer and pirouetted daintily to the beat of a tambourine. He smiled.

When he was a lad, his nursemaid, Petrona, would take him to see the dancing animals at the markets. The old woman had been perhaps his

46

one and only friend, taking him with her whenever she could. At the market, they would buy herbs for her salves and medicines, spices, nuts and sugar loaves, and she always made sure that they stopped to watch the dancing bears.

"Just for you," she'd say, but in truth, she enjoyed them as much as he did.

Over the years, he had wondered whether she knew of Eduarde's pastimes and used this as an excuse to keep him safe. At that age, he was grateful for even a moment of kindness from anyone who would give it to him. He winced. What a stupid, pathetic child he had been.

He stood there, watching the bears and feeling a lifetime away from the little boy and his old servant. A knot in his stomach twisted as memories of her fate came flooding back. The potions had killed her, though, so it didn't matter what he had accidentally said, or to whom. She had been making remedies for years. Everyone knew that, not just him. It was her own damned fault she got caught.

Old Petrona's auto-da-fé was the first he had ever attended. The square was crammed with people from all walks of life, nobility to peasant, all vying for a better position to watch the latest group of heretics burn and blacken at the stakes. The crowd was merry with laughter as children, having gathered extra sticks, threw them on an already growing pile of faggots and tinder. The aroma of hot meat pies cut through the cool October air as the crowd settled themselves for a day of merriment and feast. His father brought the wagon so that they could be better able to see above the crowd. Because Petrona was a servant of his father's household, it was imperative that they be seen up front and center. It was a clear warning to the rest that heresy and witchcraft would not be tolerated lightly in the de Beynac household.

He was five, and the crowd and noise scared him. As he tugged on his mother's skirt, he tearfully told her he didn't want to watch Petrona die. Tucking his face into her side, he hoped to remain hidden until it was all over. Still, he could hear the crowd hush and the accusations read for the five accused. He covered his ears with both hands and buried his head deeper, but his father roughly forced his head to face the bound woman. Petrona was in the center, her head limp to the side and her hair shorn. All those with her had their hands tied behind them. The faggots were lit, there was an explosion of yells and whoops, and as the flames took hold, the crowd went even wilder as people cheered and strained their necks for a better view. Threatening him with a likewise fate, his father forcefully held his head to make sure he watched every moment. The memory was seared into his brain--the acrid odor of burning flesh, the crowd, the noise, Petrona writhing in agony, and finally his father's smile of approval that he did not turn away. So he watched her burn and was angry because she had made him cry and earn him a slap for being weak. Deep inside, though, there was a little boy who would miss her kindness and those dancing bears.

Shaking off old ghosts, he began looking around the gathering onlookers and played a game with himself. These fairs attracted all manner of men and women. It was a simple matter of watching their natures to know who was guilty and who had nothing to fear. With this in mind, he watched a ragged youth who averted his eyes. He was guilty of something that was for sure. Young men who disappeared too quickly within the crowd were obviously pickpockets and thieves. The young maids who tried to catch the eyes of the young men were sluts and whores.

Just as his thoughts were turning elsewhere, two maidservants, baskets-in-hand, rudely brushed by forcing him to step aside quickly. The gangly one was lost in a litany of complaints about her mistress, as she talked to her short, fat companion, and obviously didn't care who was there to listen.

"He's a complete stranger, I tell you, and who has to take care of him, but me. I'll tell you, though; I've been fattening my eye with bits of pottery and pewter. Why the linen alone would be worth a fine dowry to the right man. Besides, I've earned it, and no one will be the wiser when she's gone."

The fat one snickered. "Which, given her age, can't be too much longer."

This got quite a giggle from the two. Renier almost moved on, but at the last second decided to feign interest in a skein of wool and listen for a few moments more. He was glad he did, for the taller one continued in a lower voice.

'I'll tell you something as well. She's been writing. I've seen her.

She thinks I don't notice, but she's been scrawling something in her room 'till the wee hours. The woman can read and write; an unusual ability for the likes of her, if you ask me."

Her friend, eyes wide, nodded in agreement. "You've got to be careful. A woman that reads and writes is dangerous business indeed. A girl's got to do what a girl's got to do these days. Take the linen, Favia. Old India sure as hell won't need bedding where she's going."

At the mention of India's name, Renier jolted to attention and stared at the two young girls. India. He had heard that name before. Suddenly realizing that someone was listening, the two women quickly moved off into the crowd. By the time Renier had realized the significance of who India was, they were no longer in sight. India. Could it really be her?

He was eight. He and Eduarde had joined his grandfather and father at Montségur, the last Cathar stronghold, in the final months of the siege. His mother had begged his father to not let him go. He was too young, too sensitive, she said, but his father insisted despite her tears. The boy was mollycoddled, a baby. He needed toughening up, and he had silenced her tears with the back of his hand. "If the whelp starts seeing what real men are like, he'll start acting like one."

It was the last day. The fortress had been breached and soldiers and monks were everywhere. There was a spirit of celebration within the Crusader camps, and everyone was busy either in anticipation or preparation for the burnings. Camp followers, families and onlookers had already staked out the best seats and were busy socializing as they kept themselves warm with blankets and cloaks against the brisk March air. At least they'd be warm once the faggots were lit. Loud thuds echoed through the morning's mist as hammers met wood, and a large barricade took shape on the flat of the hill. The mood was lighthearted. Jests and laughter were commonplace as men slapped each other on the back and anticipated returning home to a warm hearth, with a full belly and coin for their trouble.

Renier was tired and hungry and wanted them to get on with it. That's what he was there for anyway. By now he had already been present for a number of heretic fires, but none as large as today. This time, though, would be different. This time there would be hundreds, all in one massive bonfire, and he was here to see it for himself. He was a little giddy at the thought and proud that he had been allowed to join the men. Back home he would be able to join in the conversations. People would ask him questions, and he would answer with authority because he had been an eyewitness to God's holy work.

There was a morbid attraction at the way the Cathars walked so willingly to their deaths. He was often impressed at their seeming lack of fear and wondered what they thought of as they faced their last moments. What secret did they hold that made man, woman and child face a horrible death with what only could be described as rapture on their faces? He imagined himself in the position that he had seen countless of others in. Could he do it? He watched as the older boys rough and tumbled by the barricade, threatening to throw each other in. He reminded himself not to get too close lest Eduarde push a little too hard. It was only natural to know fear.

It was cold, and spots of crusted snow still clung to dead wheat stalks. The burnings would not be for several hours yet, and he was bored. Following the natural path of the trees, he wandered a little, and then walked farther towards a crop of rocks and underbrush where he discovered a small trail. Curious as to where it might lead, he carefully climbed over a large boulder and followed it until he found himself blocked by an overhang and a stand of bushes. Petulant, he began to kick away at the hardened ground and some loose rocks—stupid heretics, stupid fires, stupid father. Unfortunately, Renier did not see Eduarde until he was upon him.

Renier knew the moment his brother moved towards him what was to come. He had the glazed eyes, the sneer, and the look of a predator that had caught his prey.

"Drop your drawers, little brother," Eduarde cooed. "Turn around now. Come on, little girl. Don't make me chase you. You know I won't be nice if you make me do that."

Renier tasted his hot salty tears. He heard his whimpering voice and felt the knot of anger and helpless frustration welling up in his stomach. He did what he was told, gritted his teeth through the pain and let his brother finish, wiping himself off afterwards. It was always the same. He promised himself that when he became a man he would kill Eduarde.

When his brother had left, he pulled up his trousers and rolled himself into a little ball, laying silent, wondering whether he would even be missed.

A small movement attracted his attention. Picking up some small rocks, he began to throw them at what he thought must be a grouse in the bushes. After a handful of stones did not flush out his quarry, he stepped forward to have a closer look. To his surprise, a young man, who at first glance seemed to be in his twenties, looked back at him. This was confusing because his clean face determined he was not yet old enough to sprout whiskers. A drab brown hood covered flaming red hair that peeked out from underneath, but what caught his attention were the young man's intense blue eyes—eyes that revealed he had seen everything.

Crouched down and well hidden by the underbrush, the youth looked exhausted. At first, Renier thought he was one of the stable boys, but when his cloak slipped off his shoulders revealing the shape of a small breast underneath, he realized his mistake. A leather sachet was by her side, and she grabbed it protectively. She looked like a rabbit caught in a trap. She looked the way his mother always looked moments before his father's hand reached her. She looked like he did whenever Eduarde found him.

And then the stranger did a curious thing. She smiled, and for a brief moment he felt safe. She was a victim just like he was. Putting her finger to her lips, she controlled him with her extraordinary eyes, and he willingly complied. Looking around and seeing no one else, she relaxed a little.

"I'm Renier," he said, thoroughly enjoying his own adventure.

"My name is India," She replied in a gentle voice. At that, she stood, took his hand in hers, and said, "Peace be with you, young Renier. Keep to your lips, and I will keep to mine. Remember, the dogs may bark, but the caravan goes on."

In an instant, she was gone, leaving him standing alone to wonder whether he had encountered one of the specters old people were always going on about.

Returning to camp, he found everyone busy gathering dry wood for the pyre, and he quickly got caught up in the excitement. They had already lit the faggots and were parading the heretics down to the field.

Finding a bit of higher ground with other children, he watched, fascinated, as two hundred and twenty men, women and children walked silently to their death, while the monks sang Veni Creator Spiritus.

It was not until the next day that he even mentioned the stranger to his grandfather. Even Renier could not have predicted his anger. Subconsciously, he traced his finger across a long scar that ran the length of his cheek. It was a reminder of his grandfather's blade and a hard-learned lesson about letting a heretic survive, particularly one who had escaped with the treasure of Montségur.

He quickly calculated if it were even possible that this could be the same India. She would be old, that much was certain, and clearly able to read and write, for wasn't that considered important in their religion? Her longevity alone would suggest a supernatural intervention. Could it be that after all this time the Cathar treasure could be so close? Perhaps even the grail itself? He thought of how jealous Eduarde would be at his exalted position. He was in no hurry to return to Paris and could easily make discreet inquiries. Carcassonne was beginning to hold so many possibilities.

He should be getting on, but first he had certain needs to attend to before he settled into the Cardinal's palatial abode. All this thought of power, money and India had left him unsettled and needy for an outlet. Eying a dirty little scamp all alone in a dark laneway, he headed towards him. He liked them young.

Chapter Eight

As Renier entered the threshold of the great hall, he nodded an appreciative smile to the Cardinal. It was polite, after all, to acknowledge one's host and his fine table no matter what one thought of the man himself. The chamber, from his viewpoint, presented a very pretty picture. Ablaze with candles and torches, the room reflected tongues of light that danced across the arches of grey stone, while musicians played lightly on pipes. Servants were busy heaping the tables with platters of game and fish, pyramids of fruit and nuts and flagons of good red wine. The tables, draped in white linen, were set with ewers of beaten silver and pewter plates that glinted in the torchlight. Fires blazed in wide chimney hearths, and sheepskins had been laid under the tables to warm the feet. One could not help but envy the man's wealth and admire his attention to detail. The Cardinal had it all, wealth, power and a family name. What did he have? The Papal blessing for his Holy work. For now.

In truth, he had never trusted His Eminence. He was from these Provincial parts and Renier suspected he was too lenient in his spiritual guidance with relatives and wealthy friends. It was well documented that the heresy infection could be found in all levels of society. Several distinguished guests were already deep in conversation and only a few looked up to see that it was Renier who entered. He tilted his chin higher and sniffed. He was simply a visible reminder to them that underneath their fine clothes and costly jewels they were all sinners inside. High born they might be, but they all begged the same way under torture.

He was seated on the lower half of the table, an indisputable slight by his host and an unspoken acknowledgement of their mutual distaste for each other. So be it. But he was equally dismayed to see that he had been seated next to an oaf of a cloth merchant named Raoul d'Agis. They had met on his last visit, and although the man was quite wealthy, he considered him to be an uneducated bore. He prepared himself for what would obviously be an irritating evening.

D'Aglis immediately broke off a discussion with his wife who seemed to be visibly at odds over Renier's presence. Raoul patted his wife's hand, while he mumbled something under his breath. Obviously, she disagreed.

"Raoul, do not pat my hand like I have no brain," she said crossly. "Like I don't even know what an inquisitor does." Although she lowered her voice, she was about as quiet as a fishmonger. "It's the very Burghers you deal with that they're after. Don't say a word. Not a word. He's hunting for tinder that one."

Her husband, already half in his cups, dismissed her concern with a wave of his hand and another swig of wine. He looked around to catch Renier's eye with an apologetic smirk.

"Women, what feeble-minded delights they are, eh?" Patting his wife's hand as if she had never scolded him, he rambled on. "Men understand business, do you not agree, sir? Women have no sense of business, no sense of business at all."

Renier disdainfully reached for his sachet as if to ward off any residual offending odor left from the verbal encounter and looked away. Sipping his wine in righteous satisfaction, he took note of the gentleman to his right. It was his scrupulously clean hands that first caught Renier's attention and admiration. High born. Obviously nobility. He could tell this by his high forehead, long aquiline nose and strong jaw line, but he also saw from the fraying edges of his sleeves that he lacked money. Interesting and useful information. Obviously, the fellow would need to marry a rich woman in need of his title, but from his pretty manners that might be all she would get from him. He smiled. There was an air of desperation about this fellow that he found attractive, maybe even a little dangerous. A kindred spirit perhaps?

"Sir, let me introduce myself, I am Renier de Beynac."

The gentleman nodded and returned his smile. "The pleasure is all mine, sir. I am Prades del Cros. I, of course, have heard of your Holy work and support you completely. I take it that you are here on 'official' business?"

"Let's just say, shall we, that although I am not here in any official capacity, the Lord's work never rests. I am His beloved servant, and ever at His service.

"Del Cros. If I recall correctly your family name is old and from this area?"

"Yes, my family has been in the Langue d'Oc for many generations and is proud to be loyal, faithful and devout Christians. My esteemed ancestor was Arnold Amaury who distinguished himself in Béziers."

Renier dismissed the obvious concern with a wave of his hand. "Of course, Prades. I am aware of your Vatican connections and your family's devout faith. I have never heard otherwise."

Catching Renier's gaze at his ragged sleeve, Prades added, "You may also have heard that as of late, we have hit on hard times. My father, you may well already know, was in complete support of His Excellency, and contributed more than was financially feasible to the crusades so that when he died ..."

"He left you and yours with more debt than credit. Is that not right? And you are here del Cros ...?"

Prades cast a crooked smile. "To do what I must, sir. Show my face and find a rich bride. I will marry well and restore my family's wealth as is my duty." He picked up his wine, and with a nod and a broad smile, he toasted everyone and anyone around him.

Renier was delighted and intrigued. Slowly putting down his wine, he glanced up and locked eyes with Prades, seeing opportunity staring him in the face. Providence was within his grasp, and in that moment, he had a brilliant plan. A little added gold in Prades' empty pockets would secure his attention and his silence.

"Perhaps, Prades," he said, measuring his next words with care as he poured his new friend more wine, "I can be of help to you. In fact, we may be of help to each other. I presume, being from these parts, you are aware of the Cathar heresy?"

"Of course, sir. My father and grandfather both fought alongside Montfort. The Cathars were a curious sect to be sure, certainly one with strange beliefs. What is one supposed to think of those who consider the earth to be hell? There can only be one answer, and that is that they have been taken over by Satan himself. As far as I know, though, they have been completely eradicated for at least thirty years from these parts."

"For the most part, yes. From time to time, we still find one or two hiding out, or the need to save simple folk with impressionable minds from small outbreaks of heretical thoughts. Weeding out the diseased roots in the Lord's garden is a never-ending concern when it comes to saving souls. You are also familiar then with Montségur?"

"I am aware that Raymond de Péreille, and his cousin, Pierre-Roger Mirepoix, refortified a castle that was perched on a mountain top and it became the *domicilium et caput*, the center of Cathar activities. Later, it became their refuge and the fortress was finally taken after many months. Over two hundred Cathars were burned en masse. It was a very good example of how fearsome Satan's evil intentions can take root in the susceptible minds of peasants. It was a great victory for God's army."

"That's all you know? Come now, del Cros, are you saying you've not heard other stories surrounding the fortress?"

"Yes, of course, I have. Some believe the Cathars were the keepers of the Grail. It's well-known that the walls were taken down brick by brick in search of the fabled Cathar treasure, but none was ever discovered."

"Never discovered, my friend, because four Cathars escaped over the walls the night before. Never found because my father's spy was brutally murdered before he could name those involved. I was there, Prades, and I know something that none of them know." Renier took a drink and raised his eyebrows to gauge his new friend's reaction. Desperate men were always so attractive.

"I see before me, Prades, a man that is both intelligent and a devout Christian; one that perhaps for the right price would be willing to, oh, how shall I put it? Partake with me in a Holy quest?"

His prey raised an eyebrow and etched the lip of his cup with an immaculate finger. "If you are referring to recovering the treasure taken from Montségur, I must say that I'm intrigued, more than interested. Consider me your man."

It was like taking candy from a baby. Renier took a drink and smiled.

"M. del Cros, a toast, for we have an accord. You are, of course, aware of my station and power, and aware of what might befall someone who betrayed my confidence and trust?" He hesitated and lowered his eyes. "No matter what." Renier waited until his words hit home.

The slight nod of acknowledgement brought satisfaction.

"Good. Then listen well, for I am interested in hunting down an old woman. I know not where she lives or what she looks like, but her good name is India. She lives here in Carcassonne near the market, and her servant's name is Favia. Find her. I want to know everything about her. How long she's been here, who her family is, where she lives. Do you understand? Everything. No one is to know anything. Not a word. I strongly advise you to remember that, and you will be a very rich, very happy man."

Prades del Cros turned fully and looked Renier straight in the eye. "I understand you completely. Shall we toast?"

Pewter plates of roasted fowl and well-seasoned fish were put before them along with trenchers of warm fresh bread and more flagons of wine. The hall was filled with laughter and chatter, boasting and song. Four shapely dark women, enticingly draped in multi-colored silk scarves, danced throughout the hall to the lively tune of a wooden flute and the beat of drums. Renier smiled. He was content with so much more than a full belly and a new and interesting friend. Finally, at long last, he had an opportunity that promised power and wealth and the world at his feet. Del Cros would be a problem, but no matter; he'd take care of him later.

Chapter Nine

Wringing a cloth and wiping Jourdain's wound, India looked around the sparse room. The well-oiled linen stretched tightly across the windows let in a dimmed soft light from the morning sun. Her gaze fell to the floor. Favia would need to tend to the rushes later on that day. The marketing and water she could fetch before the noon sun, and on her way, she could also purchase some feverfew and nettle. Briefly, she thought of a small herbal mixture that helped pain and tried to remember the exact combination. Jourdain was now rising a little more each day, but he still tired easily, and although he denied it, visibly winced when he turned.

"How's the pain today?"

"Much better, thank you."

India grunted. She had noticed his awkward, compensating movements and carefully began to re-bandage and poultice his wound against infection. She was not taking any chances.

They had managed to send word to Maura via other merchants that he would return safely in the next few weeks. Not wanting the poor woman to worry, she had made the message brief with little detail. There would be plenty of time for explanations later.

Finishing the wrapping, India sighed and placed the used strips of linen onto an old wooden tray. "Ah, Jourdain, I should have liked to know you when you were a young boy. I would have enjoyed watching you play. I had no time for children in my prime, but I've mellowed over the years. It has only been in my later life that I have truly embraced my faith and truly understood what it means to be a Believer."

Jourdain smiled. "This faith of yours, I have heard so many stories.

58

It's impossible to know the difference between truth, myths or lies. I would like to understand a little better, though, as to why the Vatican considers your beliefs such a threat."

India shook her head. "An excellent question, Jourdain. In its simplicity, our only crime is that we lived more honorably than the clerics and presented too much competition for the Roman church. Others heard that we held objects and information detrimental to the beliefs of the Christian faith and were guardians of a great and sacred treasure associated with an ancient knowledge. Their fear of us was, in part, caused by our knowledge of the bloodlines of Jesus and the Grail mother, Mary Magdalene.

"We didn't stand a chance no matter what we did, no matter what we believed, and no matter what we held sacred in our possession. Even the Christians in our area were angry and frustrated, for to take our side was certain death for themselves and their families. For those who wanted wealth and lands, it mattered little about the faith of the people from whom they stole. For those who wanted treasure ...well, that's another conversation we shall have later." She stopped talking for a moment and tilted her head towards Jourdain. "Are you up for a short walk? If so, come with me to the solar. The walk will do you some good, and we can chat there in private."

"I'd like that; at least, I'd like to try."

"Good. You'll have to help yourself up. I'm not likely to be much use for stability."

Jourdain weakly followed India's shuffled steps to a large room where a comfortable hearth fire blazed under an ornately plastered chimney. The dark, narrow windows were fitted with oiled parchment and much of the room's illumination was from the hearth. Upon the walls were hung colorful panels of linen cloth, some dyed, some embroidered. In the center, there were two comfortable-looking padded chairs placed upon a carpet, a marvel of reds, blues and gold woven into floral designs.

Looking around the room in amazement, he didn't catch her next words and had to ask her to repeat them.

"I said to sit yourself here near the fire to keep warm. The rain from last night made the house damp, and I don't want you to catch a chill."

"This room is beautiful, Madame. The tapestries, the carpet ..."

"Yes, yes, beautiful things indeed, but still things of this earth. You asked to know a little more of my faith, and I shall tell you. The truth, however, is far more complicated than you know."

"We are alone, then?"

"Yes, yes. Favia's busy at the market likely telling her little friend about old and crazy Madame. She'll be gone for a while. You look nervous, but relax. I tell you only words. There is no one else to hear, and all that I tell you will only be known by you, for everyone else is long dead. What you do with my words, my dear, will be your legacy. I leave them all to you."

"My concern, Madame, is for both of us, and as you well know, words can cause all manner of danger."

"True enough, Jourdain. True enough."

Settled comfortably now in her chair, India took a minute and thought back over the years, to her childhood and the chain of events that shaped her life and its purpose. There was so much to tell.

"That which is born of the flesh is flesh; that which is born of the Spirit is Spirit. Do you know of this saying?"

"I believe it's from the New Testament; is it not in The Gospel of St. John?"

"Very good, Jourdain, I'm impressed. It is indeed from the Gospel of John, 3:6 to be precise, but what do you suppose it means?"

"Well, that things of the earth are of the earth and that of spirit belongs to Heaven."

"What that saying means to a Believer, or credente, is that there are two powers in the universe, a good God that dwells in pure Spirit and Light, and another, Rex Mundi, the god that is entirely evil and rules over the World of Matter."

"The World of Matter, meaning the Earth?"

"Precisely. That is why these things around you, this carpet, my pewter dishes, this house, treasure, wealth and power have no spiritual value. They were created by the evil god, Rex Mundi. What's more, within each individual lies a shard of the Divine Light, the Angelic Soul that has been trapped in a "garment" of flesh by the dark angel Lucifer. Because we are confined here on earth, in our 'garment of matter,' our

60

soul has forgotten its origins with God. We are therefore doomed to reincarnate time and again, until through a process of purification, we are finally able to return to God."

"I see. This is why, then, so many walked willingly to their deaths, to return to God?"

"Yes. To a believer, the Christians offered a way to immediately return to spirit through self-sacrifice without the need to reincarnate future lives."

"You would have done this as well?"

"I had a different path to walk. Souls can take many lifetimes to reach perfection before their final release. I believe this could be my fate."

"Tell me, what was it like before?"

"I can only tell you what I have been told myself, for I have never known a time that we were not hunted. In the days of my grandparent's youth, Langue d'Òc was filled with many different cultures and religions because the Crusade had not yet touched them as it had in my time. The mountains separated them from all that was evil in the outside world and allowed Jew, Muslim, Christian and Cathar to work and worship side by side. It was a time of peaceful co-existence. Our troubadours, famous and respected, composed long lyric poems of joie, jovens, and valors, and traveled far and wide reciting their works. Our langue d'òc, the language of yes, was rich and passionate and imitated in all the high courts. Women, married or single, owned property, and among Noble families it was the custom for one of the daughters to be fully ordained as a priestess. Our local law of "Partage" established equality and dignity among all people. What we had created in our protected region was how people were meant to live--together in peace and harmony. These were the true teachings of Jesus and his wife, the Magdalene, who believed in the eternal balance between male and female, dark and light, earth and spirit.

"You believe Jesus to have been married?"

"Of course! Jesus and Mary Magdalene were man and wife. They already had twin boys before the execution. Afterwards, Mary fled for safety's sake into Egypt where their daughter, Sarah, was born. Later, when even Egypt was no longer far enough away, they fled into Langue d'òc where their descendants live to this day."

"I think I see why Christian and crown considered your religion to be a threat. These ideas are very different from the Christian faith that believes Jesus to be divine. What you are saying is that Jesus was human. On what truth do you base this?"

"Jourdain, I have already confessed my Cathar faith to you. I wish this was the greatest of my secrets to tell, but it is not. Before I answer your last question, there is something I must first tell you. I fear this disclosure to you more than anything else."

Jourdain leaned forward and smiled. "You may trust me, India. I owe you my life. I will not fail you; this I promise."

"Had I known what horrors lay ahead, I sometimes wonder if I would have had the strength to carry on. The screams of the others still haunt my dreams and echo into each of my endless dawns. The stench of burning flesh is forever embedded in my pores. I saw no compassion in Montfort's legacy, but only a glazed fervor that came second to frenzied greed, and a pope and King that allowed the crusaders to kill all whom I loved. For years, I resigned myself to give my life at any moment, but death took me not. Is it not ironic that I, who so wanted to die for valor, was chosen to live?" India laughed nervously. "Forgive me, Jourdain, I am rambling again. You know of Montségur, do you not?"

He nodded. "I have heard the stories."

"I was certain you would have. Your parents, did they ever speak of your birth?"

"Only that they had been childless and God had blessed them with a gift ..."

For a moment, she felt dizzy and hesitated, pressing her fingers into the chair's arms to regain her focus.

"My gift, Jourdain. You were my gift. I gave you to your parents."

He stared incredulously. "How can that be?"

"It can, and it is. You were born with a cross patois mark on your left shoulder, and there is no doubt that you are the child I gave up."

"I'm sorry; I'm confused."

"Let me explain everything. You were conceived at Montségur. I was there, as was your father. I, a Cathar, and your father, a nobleman and Knight Templar, had a love affair that in any other situation, would have never been approved. This tale is just the beginning of your legacy."

A loud bang instantly brought them to silence. Hand raised, India cocked her head, waiting until either further noise confirmed Favia's return or she could identify the source. Stifled cries from the marketplace echoed through the walls, but nothing further was heard.

Jourdain rose to check.

India shushed him back down. "She won't be back yet. Sit. No doubt you've had a bit of a shock, but I knew of no other way to tell you and time is running out to explain other far more important things."

"I am truly at a loss for words."

"Then say nothing and listen only."

A second bang confirmed that they were not alone, and Favia's clumsy steps up the stairs confirmed the fact. India put her finger to her lips.

"Shhh, we shall talk more tomorrow for your parentage is the least of my tale."

Chapter Ten

Mémoires de India Serras

According to our Cathar beliefs, only those who have the strength to renounce our corrupted world attain the spiritual state required to reach God. Many people, once they had raised their families, became Perfects or priests, choosing to live a hard, monastic life travelling in pairs while doing their ministry.

In my twenty-second year, my father chose to spend his last remaining time attaining this perfection. Seventeen members of our community would join him. The hidden location where we were to gather was quite a distance from our home, so my father and I had taken the precaution of arriving in the area a few days earlier. We were to stay at the home of Arnal Martel, a friend of my father's, where some of the others would meet later.

It was barely dawn in early October when our horses picked their way through the rocky trail along the mountain path. The air was crisp and cool, and the hint of a wispy mist hung low to the ground, giving the forested heights a mystical quality. In such serenity, one could almost forget the grave purpose of our journey. My wool cloak was wrapped tightly around me to protect me from the early morning chill, while my father plodded on ahead, seemingly oblivious to the frost in his rough muslin jerkin.

For a full day we rode, stopping only briefly in the afternoon for some bread and cheese. I knew that I would not be returning with my father, and we spoke of the past and what was to become of my future. Although my father had left me ample funds to carry on, I knew that from this day forward, I would be responsible for myself, and my life would never be the same.

Neither he nor I spoke idly, for we were mindful that the situation could change at any moment. Although my father tried to allay my fears, he was as alert as I was to any unusual noises. There would be no rest or sigh of relief until we safely reached our destination.

After dusk, I was terrified. Unnamed shadows threatened to leap out at us from behind each tree. Finally, travelling with only the moonlight to guide our way, we arrived at the home of my father's friend. The dim light through the window was warm and welcoming, but at that moment, I knew only overwhelming hunger, relief and exhaustion.

Dismounting, my father had to steady me. After riding for so long, my legs were weak and wobbly. Upon hearing our horses, Arnal had rushed outside, while his wife peered fearfully from their front door. Although we were expected, in those days one could never be too sure, I could hear the relief in his voice when he calmed his wife with the news that it was us.

We arrived to find a large gathering of men, women and children huddled together in front of a blazing fire. Women were ladling a fragrant stew of vegetables and fish into crude wooden vessels large enough for families to share from a communal bowl. I waited impatiently for ours, for I was starving and cold.

It was only after I had finished my meal that I looked up and noticed a stranger had moved towards the warmth of the fire. He was about twenty-five years of age, obviously well bred, tall and well proportioned. His thick hair, the color of flax, hung to his shoulders, and he wore an expression of intelligence touched with humor and boldness. His nose was long and aquiline under a broad forehead. He was, in short, the most handsome man I had ever seen.

In the dim light, I saw his face, and for a brief moment, our eyes met. I was glad that the room was so dark because I found myself blushing. I was speechless. I barely noticed that Arnal had stood up, but when he gestured towards the stranger, I snapped to attention.

"Fellow believers and friends, I am at fault for not introducing you to my honored guest. Durand is the son of my old friend Philippe de Mondragon."

At this, he looked towards my father. "Durand has been entrusted with the gathering of our sacred treasures along with the safe passage of Bishops Guilhabert de Castres and Marty to Montségur. I know him to be a man of honor, a Believer, a nobleman, a Knights Templar, and a trusted friend."

Durand nodded, acknowledging Arnal's kind words amidst a sea of mumbled welcomes and smiling faces. I'd hoped to catch his eye again, but a man's voice from the dark shadowed corner spoke above the crowd.

"What news then of Montségur, Durand? We hear that Pierre-Roger Mirepoix has become the co-seigneur and commander of Montsegur Castle and has begun to organize its defense."

"Yes, what you've heard is true. He's brought with him a complement of knights and men-at-arms who patrol and fortify the approaches to the stronghold. The fortress is on top of a massive limestone rock called the Pog. Many Cathars are starting to move to this area, and huts are being built on the eastern slope. They are boasting that they have stores of grain, rye, corn, oil and dried fish, and a cistern in the inner courtyard as large as three men across. Even Pierre-Roger himself has participated in plotting and aiding in various rebellions around the area."

Another man asked, "Can it possibly be as bad as they say? We have all dealt with these petty annoyances of wars and sieges. Our lands get burnt, and we begin again. Surely, this will soon run its course and be over."

Durand wheeled around in frustration, "Fools! This is no inconvenience. Do you really think I would walk away from my Templar vows if I did not truly believe that this is serious? The King means to eradicate all of us, and all that you have worked for. This war is about money, power, greed and fear, and I will fight to the death to protect my land and those I love."

Guilhabert stood and quietly placed his hand on Durand's shoulder.

"Peace, son. I understand your anger, but it is not through anger that we will survive. Only through love and wisdom can we overcome this darkness. To anger is to give into evil."

He slowly looked around the room. "As you know, all of us have inside ourselves both light and dark: the capacity for heights in beauty, depths of deception and the ability to misuse power. Only when we recognize these parallel energies within ourselves, will we truly become the divine beings we were meant to be."

Durand only shook his head in frustration and sat down.

"With all due respect Guilhabert, when the last Cathar is burned on the stake, who will be left to tell the truth?" he asked.

The man who had spoken before nodded his head in agreement, and added, "He speaks the truth. We have become a dangerous challenge to the policies of Rome and those of the French kings who feel that their power is being eroded. Even the priests do not do their duty. They do not instruct their flock as they should, and all they do is eat the grass that belongs to their sheep."

Another man stood up and looked around the room. "Forgive me, Bishop, but we are simple people here with simple thoughts. It is common talk that there are four great devils ruling over the world. The lord Pope is the major devil who we call Satan, the lord King of France is the second, the Bishop of Pamiers the third, and the lord Inquisitor of Carcassonne, the fourth. We are frustrated knowing that those we love, and perhaps even ourselves, will die because the French want to recoup their losses and steal our land and property."

The Bishop stood and raised his hands to quiet the group. "Listen! To lower ourselves to act the same as these devils is to place our own souls in jeopardy. To focus on power, lands and creature comforts is to entrap our souls in this physical experience."

Most members of the group lowered their heads and nodded in agreement, but some, including Durand, showed frustration.

They spent the rest of the evening talking about the Templar position. Apparently, many of the French Templars came from noble families with Cathar leanings and had been recruited from this area. They knew these people, had family in the Languedoc and were sympathetic to their beliefs, so they refused to take part in the Crusade. Durand was one of them. I knew then that we were kindred spirits, for he spoke my truths, felt my passion and expressed my anger and frustration.

67

As I listened into the night of the horrors that would soon be at our doorstep, I only grew angrier. I wanted to run and hide with the others who, even now, were fleeing to live in the safety of the caves in the surrounding hills. I wanted Durand to notice me. I wanted to grow old. I wanted to love without fear. But those things seemed to be a young girl's dream that would never be.

That night we slept where we could, with women and children given warmer places nearer to the fire. I lay as close to Durand as I dared, but I couldn't rest. My heart beat so loud that I thought he could hear it, and I kept my eyes open just to watch him breathe. I was terrified that he would open his and see me, but I wanted to remember every second that I was in his presence. Suddenly he stirred, opened his eyes and looked straight at me. I panicked and immediately squeezed mine shut. I could feel him watching me as I desperately tried to pretend to be asleep, but I finally gasped for want of air. I had been found out and wanted to die of embarrassment. But, as I slowly looked over in his direction, I relaxed and smiled. Although his eyes were tightly closed, there was a lopsided grin on his face. I dreamt of that smile for the rest of the night.

* * * *

The next morning, I awoke to the clatter of a large pot being brought to the hearth. I hopefully looked around for Durand, but he had obviously risen with the other men. Stretching my painful muscles, I made my way to the kitchen to offer my help.

Biatris was a much younger woman than her husband and robust from years of hard country work. A sizeable woman with an intimidating girth, it was plain that there were very few things that the woman would not, or could not, tackle. She smiled as I entered the room, and came towards me to give me a large hug.

"Ah, ma petite, you must be hungry. Here, here, sit by the fire and warm yourself, and I'll get you something to warm your stomach as well." I loved this woman immediately. A little boy, who had been sitting in the corner, suddenly stood up and toddled over to where I was sitting. His thumb was in his mouth, and his eyes were round as saucers.

"Look India, I think you've made a friend. Roger, don't stare at our

68

guest, say hello. She won't bite, you know." He just stood and stared, the tiniest smile curling from his lips.

She laughed as she brought me a warm broth of cabbage and leeks. "Roger is three years old this year and still tied to my apron strings. Ah, it won't be for long, though. They grow up so quickly. One day they are babies suckling at your breasts and then pouf! They are gone." She nodded in my direction. "One day you will learn. We have a lot to do today for more will be arriving late tonight. I'll appreciate your help, for it's not often that I have access to an extra pair of hands."

In hopes of discovering Durand's whereabouts, I asked if she had seen my father.

"The men have decided to walk to the ceremony site, to make sure that all is well and safe for tomorrow. They won't be back likely until dinner, so we have the day to ourselves with no men folk to bother us. We can talk about whatever we women want to."

When I was done eating, Biatris gratefully set me to spinning, while she busied herself with replenishing the soup pot and baking bread. We chatted and gossiped like old friends. She made me laugh, and it was good to talk to another woman.

"So, India, is there a young man that has caught your fancy? Come on, you can tell me." When I blushed and said no, she simply clucked and chuckled.

"It won't be long now, ma petite. You'll see. One day he will simply walk through your door and your heart will beat like it has never beaten before. Plenty of time to take the vows and be celibate. Look at Durand's Aunt, the Count Fois' wife. Why she married and raised six children, and it was only after they were all grown that she took her vows to be a Perfect. My advice to you, little one, is to find love while you're still young enough to appreciate your body~and his. And speaking of Durand, he's a fine looking young man don't you think?"

My face flushed, and when she glanced my way, she sputtered with laughter.

"I can see for myself, that you've already noticed. Well, now that he's no longer a Templar, perhaps he'll be thinking of catching up on all the female company he's missed."

It was senseless to pretend that I didn't find him attractive, but to daydream about anything more was too much, and I said so.

"Well suit yourself, girl. I've known Durand for several years now, and he's a man through and through. He walked away from the Templar orders because his family and his heritage need protection. It took a real man to do that. When this is over, he'll need to take a wife. Why shouldn't it be a merchant's daughter? You're pretty enough, even with that tangle of red hair." She tugged at a loose tendril and smiled. "Now let's get on with these chores. There are a lot of preparations needed for the ceremony, and between now and tomorrow, another four families will be arriving."

Chapter Eleven

Mémoires de India Serras

The ceremony was to begin after night had fallen, and we were to congregate in a cave used for a previous gathering. Everyone was preparing. The women baked round loaves of dark bread, while a hearty stew bubbled in the hearth fire. Bishop Guillaume sat outside and gathered the children around him, intent on giving them their lessons. I smiled as I listened from the kitchen and remembered my own lessons.

After we had eaten and the sun had set, our large group silently walked along the dark wooded paths. The young babes and little ones stayed behind with a few of the ladies for their noises might jeopardize our safety. Every one of us strained to listen for anything unusual. I was grateful for the imposed silence.

I'm sure, to everyone else, I must have looked deep in prayer, but the only thing on my mind was my Durand. I had caught his eye earlier and couldn't stop myself from smiling. He walked with the men at the end of our procession, and it was all I could do not to hang back just to be near him.

I have never loved the woods at night, and the winding craggy path that followed along a bare rock face was frightening. At long last, we arrived at the cave, and one by one stepped inside a large cavern. As our tapers were lit, and our dark sanctuary brightened, we looked up and were awed by a glorious sight. The ceiling of the cave had been painted in a dark blue with hundreds of golden stars everywhere. It was magic. Surely not one of the great cathedrals could even compare with its simple beauty.

Lit only by our candles, it was as if the roof was transparent and the night sky itself had chosen to participate in our honor. Adults and children both were entranced and continually gazed upward. We were surely in a holy place.

The cave filled with believers and sympathizers, while the candidates lined up and stood before Bishop Guillaume and his two assistants. Clothed in white robes with a simple cord around their waist, I saw my father standing with the others. He looked serene, happy and content. I caught sight of Durand to the left of me and for a brief moment, our eyes locked. When I turned once more to my father, I realized that he had been watching and correctly interpreted my look. I blushed profusely and hoped that Durand had not seen and deduced what my father had recognized.

Bishop Guilhabert began to speak. "You must realize that when you are before the Church of God you are before the Father, the Son and the Holy Ghost, as the Scriptures teach. For Christ said in the Gospel, according to Saint Matthew: "Whosesoever two or three are gathered together in my name, there I am in the midst of them.""

Therefore, must you learn that if you would receive this Holy Prayer you must repent your sins and forgive all men. He began to outline the obligations which the candidates were to undertake and took them phrase by phrase through the Pater Noster, the only formal prayer that Christ himself taught and the only one we recognize.

Our father, which art in Heaven,
Hallowed be thy name.
Thy kingdom come,
Thy will be done on Earth as it is in Heaven.
Give us this day our supplementary bread,
And remit our debts as we forgive our debtors.
And keep us from temptation and free us from evil.
Thine is the kingdom, the power and glory for ever and ever.
Amen.

The Bishop continued:

"Do you promise that henceforth you will eat neither meat nor eggs, nor cheese, nor fat, and that you will live only from vegetables and fish; that you will not lie, swear, kill, or abandon your body to any form of luxury; that you will never go alone when it is possible to have a companion; that you will never sleep without breeches and shirt; and that you will never abandon your faith for fear of water, fire or any other manner of death"?

One by one, the candidates denied all luxuries and vowed to never allow the fear of death to draw them from their new obligations. The candidates then prostrated themselves in veneration to Guilhabert.

I watched my father, kind gentle man that he was, proudly step forward and accept his vows. Guillaume then spoke to all.

"Go ye into all the world and preach the Gospel to every creature. If anyone strikes him on one cheek, he should turn to him the other. If anyone takes away his cloak, he should leave him his coat also. And he should neither judge nor condemn, but follow all the many other commandments which the Lord made for His Church.

"By God, and by us and the Church, may your sins be forgiven. We pray God to forgive you them."

Adoremus, Patrem, et Filium et Spiritum Sanctam.
Adoremus, Patrem, et Filium et Spiritum Sanctam.
Adoremus, Patrem, et Filium et Spiritum Sanctam.

* * * *

After the ceremony, there was food and drink in celebration, and I settled myself on some rushes beside my father who was discussing the finer points of the Gospels with Bishop Marty. Durand had disappeared somewhere, and I was a little disappointed that he was nowhere to be seen.

Caught up in a little game with some children, I didn't even notice that my father was trying to catch my attention.

"India. India," he repeated. He nodded to his side, where I found Durand sitting where Bishop Marty had been only moments before. "I would like to introduce you to someone. This is Durand Mondragon, nephew to the esteemed Perfect, Escalermonde du Foix, a lady well-known for her kindness. Durand, may I present my daughter, India."

Not believing that it was possible to blush even more, I nodded a polite acknowledgement, and as he took my hand, our eyes locked.

"How long will you be staying in these parts?" my father asked.

"Only the night" he replied, as he continued to stare at me. My aunt is expecting us, and there is much to do to prepare.

At that moment, Bishop Marty returned and requested Durand's assistance with something. I don't remember what. Nor do I remember much else of the evening, other than he had touched my hand. I looked over at my father who said nothing. He simply smiled.

The next morning, I rose early in hopes of catching a glimpse of Durand before he left. I found his party readying the horses to leave and conveniently walked over to the Bishops, who were close by, to wish them well. As I turned to leave, he looked up, smiled right at me and winked. "Wish me luck?"

My heart leapt and my cheeks flushed when he said, "Bonne chance." He nodded, and then smiled. "Take care of yourself, India Serras." As I stood there and watched him ride off, I did not ever expect to see him again.

Chapter Twelve

Favia dove both hands into a bowl of cooling roasted chickpeas and placed four good-sized handfuls into a waiting cauldron of boiling water and olive oil. Wiping her hands on her already dirty apron, she then began the tedious job of peeling the dry skins off another bowl of loose garlic cloves.

This was her favorite time of day, and she was happy to indulge herself in the enticing aromas of garlic, fresh tomatoes and the roasted chickpeas. The recipe was from her childhood, one that her mother and grandmother would make. The familiar smells always aroused the little girl in her, and she thought back to her last memory of her mother making the dish. She was eight years old and in her grandmother's hut, looking up at her mother and smiling. It was her one happy memory that blocked out all the other memories of slaps and the endless nightly groans from her mother's bed. The next day her mother was gone. She had taken off with her latest lover, and Favia was dumped at a local seamstress for employment. She never saw either of them again.

She shrugged. It could have been worse. At least she wasn't left on the street like some of the other girls. Eventually, she found employment with India and now considered that she had a good situation. There were no brats to take care of and no filthy old employer groping her in her room at night, and then tossing her out when he caught her with child. That's what had happened to her friend, a child left at the workhouse, and Selina left to peddle herself on the streets.

Favia was smarter than that. She wasn't above every now and then picking up a few extra pennies from an old man's need for a quick grope, even a quick tumble, if they had the extra coin. She didn't spend it, though. Her coins were tied up tightly in a square of dirty linen and hidden under a loose board in her room. When the old lady finally died, she'd take a few items that would fetch a good price, add that to her little stash and leave town.

She hadn't been sure about India when she first started to work for her, and it now seemed her instincts were right. She had always wondered about the old lady's need to obsessively watch the market from her window, but she had finally decided it was because India was a nosy old bitch always wanting to know everyone else's business. After today, she saw the woman in a new light.

Taking a good handful of the peeled garlic, she gently placed the cloves in with the boiling chickpeas, careful not to splash hot water on herself, and then gave it a good stir. The aroma was already intoxicating, and she hadn't even added the spices yet.

A loud knock on the door made her jump. It had arrived. Heart pounding, she raced to the door before India heard another knock and asked questions. Out of breath, she swung the door open in anticipation, and sure enough, a tattered and filthy young boy stood there holding a package wrapped in thin muslin.

"This here's for Favia."

"I'm Favia."

The scamp eyed her suspiciously.

"What are you looking at?"

"Nothin'. I just don't usually deliver to scullery maids, do I? Is it for you?"

"It's none of your dirty business. Just give it to me and shove off before I box your ears." She snatched the parcel from his hands.

He stuck out his tongue, turned and ran off.

"Little bastard."

Quickly running back to the scullery with her prize, she opened it and ran her finger across the soft blue fabric. It wasn't a dream. It had all really happened, and what's more, there was a promise of more treasures to come. Worried that her garlicky hands would rub off on the fine cloth, she wrapped the muslin back up and returned to her recipe. Later on in the privacy of her little room, she'd take out the fabric and drape it across herself and dream. Cloves. She needed cloves, cinnamon and powder forte.

Unlocking the spice cabinet, she spooned out precious amounts of each spice into a small wooden bowl, poured a measure of olive oil into another container and then added both to the boiling chickpeas and garlic, stirring the caldron as she thought back over the day. A nice little opportunity had presented itself today at the market, and she smiled to herself as she relived the excitement of it.

She'd gone to hunt down the herbs that India had asked for and then wandered through the fabric district. It was a sunny, warm day, and India had even told her to take her time. Lost in a daydream, she'd sauntered through the stalls displaying colorful bolts of cloth, shoes and hats, as she imagined herself quite the lady draped in exquisite shades of greens and blues. She took no notice of the handsome stranger until he was beside her commenting on the fabric she was admiring.

"A beautiful color, non? Very fitting for a pretty young lady."

Favia rolled her eyes. Pretty young lady indeed. More like fancy words from some local man chatting her up for a free tumble. A second look, though, told her he was not only handsome, but obviously, by the look of his clothes, nobility. She smiled back at him. Hmm. If asked, just how much would she make him pay?

"You tease me, Monsieur?"

"Tease you? Absolutely not! I would never lie to such a fresh little beauty."

"Perhaps the sun is in your eyes then. They sell hats at the next stall."

"A hat would only block my view. I am surprised, though, that such a little pretty is unescorted through such a busy market. Is there no strong male nearby to keep your maidenhead safe from wandering rogues like myself?"

At that, she blushed and smiled. She had brushed her hair and scrubbed her face that morning, and her clothes were somewhat clean. Perhaps she really was attractive? He then took her hand, and in front of everyone, gently kissed the top. Despite the snickering chuckles from the watching merchants, and her suspicion that he was rogue, she was enchanted by the compliment.

"May I introduce myself, Mademoiselle? My name is Prades del

Cros, and you are?"

She stared into his deep blue eyes and purposely tuned out the snickers and catcalls. For even just a few minutes, she wanted the attention. "Favia, sir. My name is Favia."

"A beautiful name for a beautiful girl. Tell me, Favia, do you always daydream in front of blue cloth?"

"As do most servant girls. We also daydream of enough coin to purchase that blue cloth and other pretty things or have them bought for us."

"And who, pray, are you servant for? Do not break my heart and tell me it's a rich and lusty old man."

At this, the watching merchant shook his head in obvious disgust and moved on to another interested client. Favia didn't care. Instead, she straightened out her skirts and smiled coquettishly.

"No, she's an old widow named India, but I'm always looking for better employment."

"India. That's an odd name."

"Fitting enough for an odd lady."

"And what, pray tell, makes her so odd in your opinion?"

Turning to have another look at the cloth, she shrugged. "She's just odd, that's all."

"And what would you do with this pretty blue cloth, if say, a gentleman were to buy it for you?"

"Make me a dress, so that the gentleman might want to see me in it."

"Cheeky as well as pretty, are you? Perhaps, then, you might permit me to have enough sent to your address? I'm sure I could think of some agreeable way for you to show your appreciation."

She tilted her head, smiled and swelled her breasts. "And what would that be?

Prades smiled darkly and winked. "I'm sure I can think of something. I'll take four ells of that blue cloth." Turning back to Favia, he smiled again. "And have it sent to ...?"

"The widow Serras house near le Porte Narbonnaise."

At that, he looked around, caught her eyes and nodded his head towards a dark alleyway. She needed no further enticement as she followed him around a woman selling cabbages by a rickety old cart and into a narrow lane. Ramshackle houses tilted precariously above their heads. A refuse pile had been building up with rotting meat, decaying vegetables and human waste, but neither seemed to care. He wasted no time. Lifting up her skirts, he fumbled at his breeches and plunged himself in. Grunting and groping at her breasts, he released himself in one deep push. It was all over in a moment, and he took only another minute to straighten himself out.

"Perhaps, Mademoiselle Favia, if you are as clever as I think you are, you'd be interested in making some real coin for yourself?"

"I might. What did you have in mind? I won't be whoring myself out to your friends, though."

He laughed out loud at the thought. "No, pretty, I have something else in mind entirely, and it has everything to do with your employer."

"India? What's she got to do with anything?"

"Let's just say, Mademoiselle, that I have a friend who would pay good money for any information about your odd little widow."

"Really? How much money?"

"Enough to buy all those pretty things you want and more."

"And what do I have to do for it?"

"It's easy enough coin to earn. Keep your eyes and ears open and report back to me."

"That's it?"

Circling his forefinger over the top of her breast, he smiled. "That and perhaps a little relief whenever the need comes over me."

She smiled back. She would at last put gold in her empty pockets, and she knew just what to say to ensure his trust in her ability.

"I have seen her writing in secret. Is that the type of thing you want to know? If so, then for the right price, I am certain that I could find all manner of information."

"That is exactly the type of information I want." Pulling out a lavender sachet, he sniffed deeply to detract the stench of the back alley. "And to seal our agreement, I'll steal a kiss and have that cloth sent directly."

"How will I find you?"

"Send a lad off to the Maison del Cros with word that you have something for me and when we can meet. He'll receive coin after the message is delivered, as will you. Now off you go."

Favia smiled to herself as she stirred the large pot of chickpeas. Things were certainly looking up. There would be enough chyches for dinner, and if she was careful, enough to keep for herself in the morning, unless their house guest ate it all because India insisted he have a second helping. As for M. del Cros, she'd make sure that she was as indispensable as possible. Her future depended on it.

This "Jourdain" was certainly someone to be watched as well. Why would an old lady take such a shine to a complete stranger? It just didn't make any sense. Maybe she should have mentioned him to Prades, but doling out her information in small pieces would obviously make her more money. Likely, this Jourdain was just some thief anyway. He probably recognized the old lady was ready to die and was ingratiating himself with her in order to get everything he could. India, flattered by any attention at all, was taking it all in. Still, she instinctively felt there was something more going on.

She had surmised something was amiss the minute she walked into the house and found the pair of them in the solar. They had stopped talking the moment she walked in, and she didn't like it. Now that she knew India had something to hide, she'd pay a lot more attention, gather information and secure her future. As for Jourdain, he was a sick man and she knew a little bit about herbs herself. She'd do whatever it took to ensure he didn't interfere with her opportunity, even if she had to kill to secure it.

Chapter Thirteen

Mémoires de India Serras

Every week new rumors were raised, replacing others that had surfaced only the week before. As story piled upon story, life felt precarious, like we were living at the edge of a cliff and inch by inch were being pushed off the brink.

No one openly brought attention to themselves, for just about anything was enough to bring on suspicion. One man narrowly escaped a pyre because, after an afternoon of drinking, he protested too loudly in the streets to not being a heretic. It didn't take much to attract the attention of the black robed Dominicans, ever on the alert for Satan's presence. In the end, it took many friends to make the crows realize that it had been only the ale talking.

Whispered meetings were held in dark corners, thick woods and ever-changing houses under the cloak of night. Always there was danger. Always there were stories of other towns, other cities, other Cathars who had been found out. Two hundred burned in Minerve, another forty-five in Aix le Bains. The Perfect Blanche was tortured and burned in the square with forty others. My family, my friends. It was only a matter of time before I would be next. Still, we gathered.

Shaking their heads with heartbreaking passion, the old ones told stories of how it used to be to wide-eyed children who only had known fear. Cathar parents questioned their future, and that of their children. Yet, still we gathered.

In Albi, the remains of a Perfect woman called Boyssene were exhumed by the black ones in order to burn her already decaying body as a heretic. But still we gathered.

Could I walk calmly to my death like the others had? Could I let them take my body and thank them for allowing my spirit's return to the light? Could I bless them as they lit the faggots and love them for screaming obscenities and laughing with glee as my charred remains released my soul from this earthly hell? I asked myself these questions daily.

Many believers were now fleeing to the stronghold of Montségur perched high on the Pog. It was so secure, they said, that only mountain goats could reach it. Everyone felt that at Montségur they could safely wait out this madness and then once again return to their lives, families and homes. We all thought that sooner or later the French King, Louis X, would run out of funds and quit the Crusade. No one dared believe the unthinkable.

A year later, when it became apparent that the situation was too dangerous, I, too, travelled to Montségur with a small group. It was decided that old and faithful friends of the family would retain the house. They were to be trusted, but more importantly, they were Catholics. The lands and homes of heretics were usually confiscated, so this gave me some assurance. My thought was that when this had truly ended, I could at least return to my home.

In a daze, I packed things away that needed to be kept safe. Knowing that anything Cathar might incriminate our friends, I wrapped precious books in leather and tied them with string. My mother's dresses, heirlooms and her jewelry, save one ring that I placed upon my own hand to keep her near, were placed in a trunk and then secretly buried in a spot known only to myself and one other. After all had been hidden or released, I blessed our house and bid it protect all that lived within. God willing, one day I would return. I did not know then that this would never be.

A great sadness enveloped me to see the death of my faith for it had so many possibilities. This earthly world belonged to the Dark Lord for we saw his servants everywhere. They were slaves to the physical and material, slaves to power, and slaves to sex, while greed ruled their dark hearts. Rex

Mundi was a jealous god, and there was no place in this world for the light of the gentle Believers. The foolish crusaders and Dominicans sought to punish by fire and sword, but in reality, they offered the Cathars freedom from earthly ties and an opportunity to return to their true divine nature.

We had all agreed to stay on the mountain passes that were unfamiliar to most. This was still dangerous, but we stood less chance of meeting the inquisitors that now freely roamed the country. As we rode away from Toulouse, I began to feel safer, which made no sense at all considering our position. In Toulouse, there were only the whispers of bad news to consume my days.

Our group was small, and as I looked around, I caught the eye of a plump woman and a portly gentleman both smartly perched on matching white ponies. The couple were traveling with us part-way because they were fleeing to Spain which was considered safer. She smiled indulgently and nudged her pony close beside me. Then, nodding her head back towards an older woman and the sickly young man accompanying her, she whispered, "Stay away from the boy," she cautioned, "you never know what you may catch."

The last member of our group was a solemn, middle-aged gentleman who kept his distance.

"He's far too into himself. Not a social man at all, though, if you're not married, he might be a good catch."

Our leader, Andre, was knowledgeable and trustworthy-a Cathar himself and a man of honor. He had been a farmer who had lived his life in the mountain countryside. His size and strength alone suggested an outdoor life of hardship. After losing his wife and baby in childbirth two years previously, he had devoted his time to helping fellow Believers.

He bellowed to our little group, "There will be no stopping until nightfall."

We rode, following only the path and Andre's lantern, until very late. Suddenly he stopped, and told us to wait. He directed his horse into a dense bush that seemed to climb directly up a mountain wall and disappeared. When he reappeared, we could see his relieved smile in the dim light of his lantern. He ordered us to follow, one by one. As I coaxed my horse through the narrow passage, I was intrigued to find an ingeniously hidden pathway behind the thicket that immediately led downward and to the right. We followed this for about another hour until he again ordered us to stop. Just ahead, in the distance, a soft glow reflected on the snow from a small shepherd's cabin.

Dismounting, Andre asked us all to remain quiet until he could verify that all was well. A few minutes later, Andre returned, smiling once again, and from the doorway a man's large figure urged us all to come in and get warm.

The cabin was small, indeed, but to our cold and starving group, it was a palace. A warm fire blazed in a chimney off to one side that almost took up one wall. Andre's family had used the cabin for years, and in these days, it had become a safe stopover for Perfects and fleeing Cathars.

Andre introduced his cousin, Faure, an older man of around 40. Large-girthed and sturdy, it was easy to see the family resemblance. I suspected this man to be a baker by trade, and as if he had read my mind's thoughts, he immediately began to produce fresh bread and a hearty cabbage soup. As he busied about, a little girl of around five, clung shyly to her father. She reminded me so much of Sophie's little boy, Roger, that I found myself unconsciously smiling.

So cold and hungry were we that our immediate intent was to forego any courtesies until warm and soundly fed.

Afterwards, as I closed my eyes in sheer exhaustion, I felt a small touch on my knee. When I looked up, I saw the sweetest angelic countenance that I had ever known. She matched my gaze evenly and gave me an imperceptible smile that shone more through her eyes and heart, than at the corner of her mouth. I was captivated. She told me her name was Amidée, and so I told her mine. Bracing herself against my knees, she looked deeply into my eyes, and said, "It's you, isn't it?"

Before I could question what she meant, Andre announced that we would be leaving just before sunrise.

Too tired to care where we rested our heads, our weary little group found comfortable places where we could and slept like kings.

* * * *

The next morning, I awoke with my muscles sore from riding and stiff from lying on the cold, wooden floor. To my surprise, Amidée snuggled close to me, and her hair tickled my nose. Faure had been up for some time feeding the horses and was in the corner discussing something with Andre.

Not long after, Andre announced that it was time to rise, and amidst the groans and coughing, we all stretched aching backs. Passing around loaves of sturdy black bread, we each ripped off chunks and prepared ourselves for another long day. The somber man sat in the corner, chewed pieces of bread and silently stared. While the boy coughed, his grandmother rubbed a smelly, greasy concoction on his chest. By this time, everyone was up and about, relieving themselves and preparing for a cold day ahead.

Amidée had awakened as well. I presumed that she and her father would be travelling with us, but once again, she walked over to me, took another long look, then purposefully returned to her father, and said, "Papa it's her, I want to go with her. It is she who will take me."

Embarrassed and bewildered at the child's outburst, I began to explain to this man that I had said nothing to suggest such a situation, but he cut me off.

"Mademoiselle, my cousin, whom I trust with my life, tells me that you are to travel to Montségur. As you can see, I am but an old man. My wife, Carmelle, died one year ago, and it is my wish to take the vows of consolumtium and become a Perfect. But what is to become of my child? I beg of you; take her with you. That way, I know she will be safe. I can give you money for her keep, and she is a good girl." The entire time he spoke to me, Amidée stood by me, looking directly into my eyes.

"Tell her papa, tell her." She demanded.

"Mademoiselle, my impatient daughter wishes me to tell you something." Two months ago, Amidée told me of a dream she had. In her dream, her mother had spoken to her. She saw her as one would see a loving angel, and therefore she was not afraid. She had come to tell her of difficult times ahead, and that she should be brave. Her mother explained to her that I must take my vows, and she would be safe in another's care. She told her that there would be a woman fleeing to Montségur, and Amidee would recognize her when she saw her. You are that woman, and

I beg you to take my child with you to safety, to be her guardian and, indeed, an earthly mother to her.

There is one other thing. Both her mother and grandmother had the gift of sight, and even at her tender age, she is already proving herself to be their equal. So you see, I cannot leave her with anyone but a Cathar. No one else would understand the gift our Lord has bestowed upon her."

What could I say? The child stared so earnestly, and Faure pleaded with eyes that, like my father, knew his destiny and accepted it. His dying wish would be granted knowing that his little daughter was safe. I knew my own feelings of being alone, and although she was a brave little thing, she was still a child and afraid. I agreed, but looked over to Andre hoping to catch some kind of affirmation that I had done the correct thing. A simple single nod was all I needed to see. I edged closer to her and gently asked, "Why did you choose me?"

She answered straight away, and her words were direct, simple.

"Because you'll survive and remember me."

Although I could feel Faure's pain on leaving his only child, I understood the decision he made.

Faure held his daughter close and talked of her mother and relatives that were no longer with them. He knew that this choice would likely mean that his life would end, but it would also mean the conscious decision to quit this physical world and rejoin spirit. Christians could never understand why one would voluntarily become a prefect knowing what lay ahead. But then they did not understand our teachings.

I watched as he tenderly hugged his young child and I wondered at the strength of such a youth. She swung her small arms around his neck and held him tightly. Turning her head as they embraced, she saw me watching her from the corner of her eyes. Calling me over she clasped my hand warmly and looked intently into my eyes. Once again, I was taken aback by their deep blue intensity. I thought of my own parents and saw myself in this child's face. Such an old soul, I thought, and I wondered at my own past life connection with this child. As I looked in her eyes, she merely smiled as if to say, I already have all your answers. This was no child.

I left their company and went looking for Andre. I found him in the stable mending a pack and I sat down on an old stump turned on end.

"Andre, I know I'm crazy to accept a child to come with us, but I feel she deserves the chance. You know as well as I do that to stay will mean death for her. That will be all she has to look forward to, if she's lucky. She is your kin. If you are concerned for her safety, say so now, otherwise my commitment stands."

Andre turned to me, lowered his head once, and then quickly looked directly into my eyes.

"India," he said, "I am honored that you would care for her as a mother."

I smiled briefly; still unsure as to what kind of responsibility I had accepted into my life, let alone a child with the gift of seeing. There wasn't a town or city in whole of France that wouldn't put her to the fires if they knew.

Andre turned and walked inside to collect the travel bags, dried bread and hard biscuits, while I continued tightening the horses' traces and saddles. I knew not what would lie ahead from that moment on. "The only one who would survive," she had said. I looked around and saw Andre walking back now with her bags. All would die. A cool breeze fell over my cheeks, and I shuddered.

Chapter Fourteen

Mémoires de India Serras

Riding through the mountains with Amidée in my embrace, my fear was so strong I could taste it. Every hill was suspect as to what lay behind, and every peak left us open to what lay beyond. I was afraid for us all. The clop, clop, clop of hooves on rock lulled us into silent thoughts of safe havens, distant lands and secluded woods. We all wanted to be any place but here, anywhere that didn't smell of death.

Dead leaves crunched under our horses' hooves, and a light dusting of snow clung to branches and rocky outcrops making the hills slippery and difficult to climb.

Concerned for our journey through the wintry mountain passes, Andre stopped occasionally to gather small dry wood for fires. What wouldn't fit into his sack he tied together and strapped to his horse and to ours. On we plodded, covering ourselves as best we could against the winter chill until reaching a small shepherd's hut at dusk. No welcoming fire awaited us, but it was dry and would suit our purposes for the evening.

The mountain paths ensured less military traffic, but, unfortunately, there were more opportunities for bandits. It was the latter that we kept a constant vigil for as our little party plodded along. The weather was cold, and the wind whistling through the rock wall along the trail made it colder still. We were all hungry and ready to stop, but each of us knew the distance we needed to travel. Biting off a piece of hard tack for Amidée, I handed the child a piece. Quietly she grabbed it, piped out a thin "merci," and sank her teeth into the hard-pressed cookie.

Finally allowing us to rest, Andre started a small fire with the tinder and dry sticks that he had gathered, while our horses nibbled at frosted dried grasses in a nearby meadow. It felt good to dismount, and I suggested to Amidée that we stretch our legs in the direction of a small hill. She was cold and tired, and I hoped that the walking would at least warm her up.

Suddenly she looked towards the hill's crest and simply stated, "She is waiting for us just over that hill."

I wondered who she was speaking about, but before I could ask she was already ahead, and I had to run to keep up.

"Amidée come back. Wait for me," I panted, but when I reached the hill's crest, I was shocked into silence.

Sitting on a stump was a weathered old woman. As much a part of the landscape as the trees, wind and ancient granites that surrounded her, there was no mistaking that she was a Holy woman for she wore the traditional dark robe and belt of the Perfect. Gradually, from hill and copse, a straggle of locals had begun to gather.

Those who arrived first genuflected in respect to her status. After receiving a customary blessing, they found rocks and boulders to sit on. Amidée was already by her side and looked back anxiously to see if I had followed. I had, of course, but she had already begun to speak by the time I arrived.

"To whoever hears these words, be thou pure, be thou earnest in thy pursuit for truth and an honorable life."

People started talking to her, asking questions, asking for blessings, kissing her hem, and one by one, they were all acknowledged. To one woman she gently smiled and replied, "Accomplish what you dream by hard work and focus. Strive for balance in all things. Believe in yourself and all will believe in you."

To a man, she answered, "Fear has no part in ruling your actions. Instead, let prudence and good judgment mark your path, for to be truly Cathar, we must have a higher understanding of our place in the world and of the duplicity of the world itself. Just as our Lord Jesus was the embodiment of the good, Rex Mundi, the lord over evil, is his counterbalance."

To another who asked about Jesus Christ, she explained, "We do not accept the Roman Christian's understanding of Jesus, but consider him rather to be the human form of an angel. Because he was already a perfected soul, he had no need to reincarnate but chose to take on a human form to demonstrate his love for humanity and to teach the way back to the light. To regain our bodies of light and angelic status, we must renounce the material self completely. Until one is prepared to do so, they will be stuck in a cycle of reincarnation, and condemned to live on a corrupt Earth."

At last, she turned to Amidée and myself.

"Come child," she said. "Let me have a look at you." Without a word or hesitation, Amidée rose from my lap and stood in front of the old woman. The Perfect did not take her eyes off her until she reached her side. Then looking up and nodding directly at me said, "You as well."

I felt like we had been summoned, and I was not sure whether it was honor or trepidation that I felt as I, too, stood before the Perfect.

"So it is you two who bring me here today." I must have looked confused for she turned my way. "You look surprised, but I tell you it is so." Her eyes now on Amidée, she said, "The little one knows, don't you dear?" Amidée's face brightened and she fairly bubbled over with a five-year-old's enthusiasm. "Yes, bonhomme, it's true. I told her you were here, and you were. I knew you would be. I knew it."

Taking my hand, the woman stared deeply into my eyes, and I was transfixed. Her eyes were the color of the winter's sea and in them; she reflected a depth and strength that I had never known. "How is it that you are called?"

After I had told her, she smiled.

"India. There are those who walk this earth always suspecting that they were meant for something more, but never finding it. That shall not be your fate, for your future is clear and etched deeply into the records. Listen well to my words, girl, for it is no accident that we meet today. From this point onwards, you must choose the path of a higher purpose and never falter from it. Yours is not the path of a Perfect, nor is it the role of wife or mother. A much greater task awaits thee, and your life will be in danger many, many times because of it.

This child beside you will be your key; the one who guides and nurtures. When you are old, it will be her name and face that you remember best. This child is gifted, and though her path will not be long with yours, united in a common love you will always be."

Amidée took my hand, and we smiled.

* * * *

As we neared the Pog's summit, we emerged dazzled by the sweeping view of vibrant green hills tumbling endlessly beyond Montségur. The radiant amber light of the late afternoon sun shone low on the horizon as we continued along the rocky path. We passed a small terraced village with many crudely built stone huts roofed in thatch or tiles beneath the towering walls of the fortress, protected on the other side by a sheer cliff. There were people everywhere absorbed in their daily chores of washing, foraging and building. Many of them nodded a welcome as we arrived. As we climbed higher, there were more rows of stone huts haphazardly perched wherever they could find purchase. A rough stone path wound its way higher until we reached a fortified wall. Catching our breath, we rested for a few minutes before we were escorted up even farther through the archway leading to the initial courtyard.

We were greeted by a young woman who introduced herself as Brigita. Hot broth was being ladled into wooden bowls and placed in our hands by an older woman.

"Welcome," said Brigita. "You can see that our numbers are growing daily. There are already a thousand of us, including the families of the Knights. Many of our householders have taken in as many as they can, but you needn't worry. We'll find you somewhere safe and dry. We're fortunate that we are still well supplied and able to keep our support lines open with the village below."

We followed her down a narrow set of steep stone steps to a small stone hut just outside the walls and tightly nestled into the hillside. I was worried about Amidée, but she was as sure-footed as a mountain goat. As we descended, Brigita informed us that we would stay with a woman named Marie. After tapping lightly on a slatted, wooden door, we were greeted by a rosy-cheeked, older woman who welcomed us with a hug and ushered us in.

"Come in, come in. I've got a nice fire going and some lentils in the pot. I'm Marie. Have you been fed? Are you thirsty? The two of you have had quite the climb today, and you both must be exhausted. I've only got one stool, but sit where you may."

We both nodded in agreement and collapsed on a straw mattress that was off to the side, while she took the stool. I introduced ourselves, where I was from and Amidée's situation. She simply listened and then with a nod and smile to my sleepy little girl, said. "Well, both you and the little one are welcome here."

Her home was a narrow, single room with a raised stone hearth vented at the ceiling at one end. A low fire burned and flickered on a tiny window where oiled linen had been stretched across and provided a small amount of diffused light into the room. Rushes were strewn about the earthen floor and a multitude of various dried herbs hung from low beams in the ceiling that scented the room. The main focus, however, was a trestle table that held three large wooden bowls, a stone mortar and pestle and a number of clay jars.

I commented on the herbs, and she smiled. "My grandmother was a gifted healer, and I was fortunate that she taught me everything she knew about arts and potions before she passed. If you have an interest, I could use your help. So many people are arriving now that I can't keep up."

Thus, learning the healing arts became my daily focus for during my first year at Montségur. Marie was a relentless teacher and made me repeat the herbs names and usage until I was dreaming of lamb's quarters, rosemary, comfrey, wild ginger, calendula, marshmallow roots and spiderwort. We mixed potions and tinctures till well into the night, then tended to cuts and bruises, childbirths and broken bones during the day. She taught me all she knew, and I was a willing student; Amidée was my little helper.

About a month into our stay, Marie ventured to a different area, where she had seen a large patch of wild garlic. She had cautioned us that it would be near a known path used by the villagers, and we should always be on the watch for mercenaries. We found the isolated little meadow without incident and spent several, pleasurable hours harvesting a large basket of thyme as well as the garlic.

Boosted by our easy afternoon, we headed back, picking our way across a narrow passageway. Suddenly, Marie motioned us to stop, be still and make no noise. Panicked, we crouched low to the ground and heard two men speaking. From the sounds of their voices, it was obvious they were quite near, possibly on the outcrop above us. I held Amidée close. A deep, husky voice was complaining that the money was not enough, and he wanted more. The other man let loose a sneering laugh and called him a fool. "How dare you suggest we pay you more? The trail you showed me was useless. We could no more get a goat up that path than an army of men."

"But I told you from the beginning, they keep the paths a guarded secret." the other man replied.

"Yes, but you promised us that you could discover them. So tell me, is this what I paid you for~an empty cave? You must be a fool to think I'd give you coin for such information."

With that, we heard the sound of a sword being released from its scabbard. Obviously terrorized, the man began to sob, begging for a little more time. There was a gurgling sound, some weak coughing and then all was silent except for the sound of footsteps walking back through another path.

Releasing a deep sigh, Marie signaled for us to stay where we were. When we again resumed our climb, our ears buzzed and burned listening to every crackle of twig and tumble of rock.

* * * *

Later that evening, still shaken from the day's event, I could not sleep. I rose to watch the moon at peace at least for this night. Wrapping my cloak around me, I silently stole away to the now dying embers of the exhausted fire in the courtyard. I sat lost in my own deep thoughts before I sensed I was being watched. I slowly looked up and gasped. I could not believe my eyes; it was Durand who stood before me.

I remember my heart beating so hard inside me I thought I would faint. I could have been anywhere on earth, and I wouldn't have noticed. He walked closer, looking at me as if I were a vision that might disappear.

Startled and embarrassed, I stammered something about being unable to sleep. I thought that he would laugh at me, or make a small light comment, but he did neither. Instead, he said nothing for a few moments, staring only at me with our eyes locked. He simply took my hand, smiled, and said, "India, I'm so glad that you're here and that you're safe."

I said something. I don't know what because all that mattered in that moment was that he had remembered my name and was holding my hand.

He had just arrived, he said, from Toulouse, bringing reinforcements. He was spending much of his time guarding another manned outpost known as Roc de la Tour, the "Tower Rock." He held my hands, rambling on in apparent nervousness.

"Right now, we're encountering the occasional skirmish, but troops are massing into the valley in an attempt to draw a tight perimeter around the fortress. We're expecting more, and it's becoming difficult for supplies to get through. Of course, with the winter snows on their way, it will be difficult for them to execute anything massive. I have to leave again, but I'll be back soon."

I remember thinking how strange life is. I had been terrified of him realizing how much I liked him, yet now I wondered if he would ever have the courage to speak what I saw reflected in his eyes.

He soon answered my question. Letting go of my hand, he moved closer and gently took my face into his hands. In the next breathless moment, he leaned down and kissed me long and deeply.

No declarations were needed, for I now knew that my Durand and I shared a common soul. I also knew in that instant, as I know now, that he would always be my partner, and I, his. It would be a bond that even death could not break.

He whispered, "Wish me luck?" I did, and as he turned away, he smiled and said, "Take care India Serras. We will see each other again. I promise."

Chapter Fifteen

After that night, encounters with Durand were few and mostly in the company of others, but just one smile in my direction was enough to make my heart race. I constantly looked to see if he was near. Opportunities for "accidental" encounters drove me crazy, and on more than one occasion caused Amidée, my constant companion, to giggle. I volunteered for anything that would put me closer to where he might be.

A few weeks later, I was instructed to gather wood along a secret footpath we frequently used in a fairly safe area. Amidée was supposed to go with me, but at the last minute, someone called her back to help with the younger ones. Elated to have some time to myself, I trudged through the snow down the well-beaten path. As always, Durand was on my mind.

The cloudless blue sky promised a day of respite from a world of fear, and I drank in the fresh beauty of the morning. The hills filled my lungs and soul with the crisp mountain air and renewed hope. For just this morning, I was safe. Twirling myself in the sunshine, my eyes closed, and I took a deep breath. I was a tree stretching my long twiggy fingers to the heavens, I was a cornflower, a buttercup, a tall pine; I was the hawk that circled above. I was a part of the whole, and it felt delicious to be alive in such a landscape.

Giving full reign to my daydreams, I fancied myself at Court. My Lord, a handsome young knight (who looked very much like Durand), bowed, and I curtseyed back. In my mind's eye, he took my hand and pressed his lips gently against my palms. "Why my Lord Durand, I had no idea ....Why yes, I would be honored to share this dance." Lifting my imagined silk skirt to the tune played by court musicians, I began to dance light, pretty steps. Well, as best as one could in snow.

It was then that I heard a man's laugh. Mortified, and already knowing in my heart who I would see, I looked around to find him sitting on a log at the forest's edge.

My cheeks blazed with embarrassment, as I stared at him, speechless. Sword by his side, he had obviously been honing his skills, for he looked sweaty, rugged, and God help me, unbelievably handsome. Dressed in black leather, his jerkin was open enough to reveal a muscular chest, manfully covered in hair. His sheepish grin acknowledged what I already suspected. He had seen, and worse, he had heard all. I wanted to melt into the very hills. I knew that he had seen me as the foolish young girl that I was, not the woman of mystery and charm that I had imagined only moments before.

As he stood up and walked towards me, hand extended, a broad smile never left his chiseled face. "Forgive me, milady. It has been a while since I have seen such passion and joy in so pretty a face," Taking my hand, he said, "There is, however, one thing wrong. A beautiful lady, such as yourself, should never dance alone."

I mutely stood there not sure what I should do. His eyes looked at me, demanding my full attention. I stammered out something about collecting wood and getting caught up with the beauty of the hills.

"Understandably so," he agreed. "These days bring so few joys." He stared into my eyes. "But when one finds beauty, it is good to celebrate it. Shall we dance?"

I looked up and smiled. He began to hum a familiar song. I joined in, and it was there in those hills, under a perfect blue sky and amidst the tall snowy pines, that we truly fell in love. As we danced, there was a quickening between us that swelled like a rising tide. It was as if the universe, knowing that our time together would be short, chose to dispense with all formal courtship.

When we were done, he glanced at his sword, and for a moment, there was an awkward silence. I thought he would leave again, but instead he took my hand into his.

Very slowly, he leaned towards me, looked deeply into my eyes, and simply said, "The truth, India, is that love, hope, the sacredness of life, are now only what we are able to make of them in the short time we will have left."

He smiled. "Come with me. There is a cave with an underground stream nearby, a sacred place where the shining ones used to pray. I want to show it to you."

Silently, I followed him through a threaded path that wound through the thickest part of the woods. The path had obviously not been used for many a long year for bushes and thickets blocked our way. But I was undeterred. I would have followed him anywhere. Suddenly he stopped and motioned to me to come and look.

Hidden well amongst the rocks and trees was a small frozen waterfall. Like a ragged crystal sheet, the water lay suspended as it flowed over its rocky banks. Sacred it must have been, for the very air stilled and hushed at our arrival. Taking my hand, we climbed over the boulders where he held thick bushes aside revealing a worn path that led to a cave well hidden behind the falls. It was magical.

I was at peace with the world and with myself, and when he took me in his arms, I melted, enfolding my spirit into his. We laughed. We talked. My heart was light, and he told me more about himself. Like most young noblemen, he had initially joined the Templars for fighting and partage and had done his family honor in the Holy Land. He had been with the order for less than five years but was well-known throughout his father's lands. Although he was a Christian Templar, his mother's family had heavy Cathar ties, and it was this discipline he honored. He had seen enough of Louis' crusade and could no longer be a part of it. His loyalty was with his family, and he would fight for what he believed.

I told him about myself, about my mother, about wanting to handle a sword. He smiled when I told him this and looked at me long with those deep blue eyes.

He kissed me again, softly, tenderly–a lover's kiss. With such intense beauty within and all around us, I gave myself willingly and fully to him. His hands shook as he undid my bodice, and his eyes questioned, but I was never surer of anything in my life.

I remember everything as if it were yesterday. His hair, his smile, his voice, his touch, and the way he looked. I remember his smell and the warmth of his body after we had laid together, our arms desperately holding onto each other. Each breath, each moment became my eternity~ my escape from a painful reminder that the day might be our last.

Sometimes, late at night, Durand comes to me in my dreams. Still the gentle lover, I can feel his caresses and soft kisses on my breast until dawn's early light awakens me to the truth of my aged body. I suppose old women charged with such holy tasks aren't supposed to talk about such things, let alone remember them, but I do.

Love is something I remember from a long time ago, an excitement in the spring air, a hint of a stolen kiss, a long passionate look, eyes locked in silence, unspoken vows and promises. For God's sake, let me say his name out loud just one more time to someone who will listen. I am so tired of whispering his name to the trees and calling his ghost from under moonlit nights.

Let me just once, before I die, speak honestly of my love and of my sorrows. I am too old to care what the truth will cost and too tired of a disguise that even these days barely keeps me from the Christians' burning pyre. It would be a blessing. Sweet death would only bring me closer to being reunited with him, so I fear it not. I was never cut out to be a helpless old woman.

Chapter Sixteen

The winter was long and harsh but except for the occasional skirmish, it was relatively quiet. Durand was ever on my mind as our love continued to grow.

I had become an accomplished healer, even by Marie's standards, something that I was very proud of, and we were constantly busy with requests for salves and tinctures.

By spring, Hugues des Arcis, fed up with the usual siege strategy of starving defenders out, gathered a military command of 10,000 royal troops at the base of the Pog.

They decided to directly attack and eventually secured a location on the eastern side of the summit where they could construct a catapult. All the refugees living outside the walls were now forced to move inside, making living conditions more difficult. Our main focus at this time was to hold the barbican, but with few knights and fighting men available, help was needed.

One afternoon, a knight came to the central square and loudly announced he needed any man or youth willing to handle a sword to step forward. Everyone looked around for volunteers, but the Perfects and Cathar Believers were pacifists and refused to participate in combat.

"For God's sake, we are down to one hundred fighting men and we can't do this alone. Is there no one who will take a stand?"

I watched as a few young men stepped forward and said they would help, although they had never held a sword before.

"No matter, lads, we'll teach you. Is there anyone else?" he pleaded.

Frustrated at the lack of response, I resolutely walked through the gathering crowd to stand beside the young men.

"I will."

The knight looked disgusted and shook his head. "It's a sad day when we need the help of a woman. Go back and sit down."

When I refused, he growled, "I said, no. Is there anyone else?"

I was about to stand my ground again when I heard Durand's familiar voice loud and clear behind me.

"She stays, and she will learn to handle a sword, even if I must teach her myself."

I turned to look at the man I loved and saw only pride in his eyes.

* * * *

My lessons in swordplay began the next day, but I also continued to help Marie for as the living conditions deteriorated, contagion and sickness increased. I was given a rapier, a smaller, lighter sword, and taught the very basics of counter-play. Durand would brook no shortcuts in my training for one slip could cost me my life. He said my short, quick steps made me a natural, but my thrusts needed to be stronger and focused on the intent to kill my opponent. I cannot say whether a sword in my hand made me more attractive, but our lovemaking afterwards during visits to our cave became more intense.

All too soon, my skills were called into practice; the barbican had been breached and needed to be defended. As a woman, a Cathar and a healer, I did not like killing another human being, but I came to understood how men's emotions got lost in the mayhem. I screamed with rage, fear and frustration as my sword plunged into a man's body, spraying me with his blood, or as I shoved mercenaries off ladders, only to hear their cries as they plunged to their death on the mountain below. For me, the attack was a blur of rage and blood, and I did not stop until I was pulled away by Durand. There were too many of them and too few of us. We had to retreat and the barbican was taken.

The trebuchet was moved closer, and under the constant bombardment, our living situation inside the fortress deteriorated even further. I did what I could to help people, but there were just too many in need and soon motionless bodies littered the courtyard.

The wooden shelters, haphazardly built barely protected ashen faces gaunt with hunger and disease as they murmured prayers over the muffled cries of infants and children. Bodies huddled beneath cloaks and ragged furs, exhausted by hunger or illness, lay waiting for death.

Kettles of boiling soup that wafted in my direction were mixed with the nauseating stench of filth, death and disease that even smoking fires could not disguise. As I surveyed the devastation of the scene, all I could do was turn my head and cry.

Chapter Seventeen

The following morning, after Favia had left the house, India requested that Jourdain follow her again into the solar. The fire had not been set, and despite the finery, the room had an edge of gloom in the dim light. Ambling over to her chair, she sat down, shifted her shawl so that it covered her shoulders and waited for him to find a comfortable position. She smiled. Like his father, he wore his worry in every line on his face.

"You're certain Favia is out? Will she be long?"

"Long enough. She's off washing garments."

He visibly relaxed. "We have some time, then. I have so many questions."

"All of which will be answered in due time."

"You look pale. Are you well?"

"I put it down to too much garlic. Just another example of how my old age is catching up with me and testing my digestion."

Jourdain smiled. "I have been thinking about what you said yesterday. Is it not miraculous that of all places I should take shelter here? This cannot be just an impossible coincidence. It's truly a miracle."

"A miracle? Possibly. As I said yesterday, it is as much of a surprise to me, but in my mind, your presence is more of a confirmation. Please, let me continue my tale. What I've already told you is the least of what is yet to come."

India sat back, closed her eyes, inhaled a deep, long breath and slowly exhaled through puckered lips. Her hand rubbed her furled brow soothing a tinge of a headache. Each word promised to cause her more pain, so she began slowly.

"I have dark, wild nights with memories that take me to the black corners of my mind. I usually pray to God to let me forget them, but now I must remember."

Her eyes remained closed, and she could feel herself transported to another place and time. Her breathing slowed, and she began softly. "The sounds of Montségur still linger, swirling and roaring in my head: clashes of steel, cries of dying men, murmured prayers of survivors, the horn of surrender sounding across the mountain peaks like the dying howl of a gutted beast. These sounds of Montségur never leave me."

India silently bowed her head for a few minutes to gather her thoughts. The familiar shift of her memory settled around her like a light shawl, despite her attempt to focus. The sounds did this. They transported her to another time. When her head slowly lifted, her eyes glassy, she was lost in the past and no longer in Carcassonne.

"I have lost weight and my monthly bleeding has stopped. I am pregnant, about three months along, as far as I can tell. I am terrified.

"A man called Doat has recently joined us. Call it woman's intuition, but I don't trust him. Wherever I go, he's there, always uncomfortably close. I try constantly to evade him, but in such cramped quarters, it's next to impossible. He frightens me, but I say nothing to Durand.

"Within days we have heard that we have been betrayed. Someone has shown the crusaders the secret path and the impossible has occurred. By the time the stronghold has been breached, the stench is intolerable, even through the chilly March air. People are sick, hungry and so exhausted they no longer have the will to argue or fight.

"Durand's leg has been badly crushed from the thigh down by a stone thrown by a trebuchet. The leg is a bloody mess and infection has set in. His raging fever is evidence that his time with me will be short.

"A surrender has been established, and an ultimatum given to us. Those wishing to renounce themselves as sinners will be free to leave and embrace the Christian faith. Everyone else will meet death on a mass pyre. Only a small handful choose to leave, while the rest of us choose the promise that our souls will rejoin the Divine light. The choice is not hard. We are already living in hell.

"The night before the surrender, Bertrand Marty, the Cathar Bishop from Toulouse, speaks to me. The elders have made a decision that will seal my fate. Four of us have been chosen to protect items that cannot fall into the Vatican's hands. The truth, they say, must be protected at all costs. The escape will not be easy for it involves scaling down the fortress walls and the impenetrable eastern flank in the dead of night.

"I steadfastly refuse to leave Durand's side. He is lying on a blood-soaked sheet, and I close my eyes to what my heart already knows. They are trying to staunch the flow of blood from his mangled limb but he is too weak. He will not live the night. But he has spoken with Bertrand and tells me the decision for me to be among the chosen four has been made and is not mine to decide."

India stared hard at Jourdain. "I hated him for that. I did not want to live without him. I hated him for the promise he made me give."

She turned her head towards the window. Her face flushed and hot tears trickled from the corners of her eyes. Her clenched fist desperately held on to the past, while her voice, thin and far away, joined the present.

"He had a knight cleave his ring in half. He said his half he would die with. The other he gave to me." Opening her hand, she stared at the broken ring. "We are one soul, you and I, forevermore bound together. Godspeed and be safe." She looked up into Jourdain's eyes. "Those are the last words he ever said to me. "What happened next is never more than a thin veil away.

"They have cut my hair quickly with a sharp knife so that the thick, fiery ends are jagged. I am disguised now as a boy–boots and leggings wrapped round and round with leather laces. My skirt has been slit for this purpose. They have found me a jerkin with a long pointed hood, the better to hide my face. They say, 'Keep your head down, make no eye contact, and talk to no one.' I am torn because I want to stay and die with the others, but I cannot. I am their memories. I will tell their stories.

"People place objects in my hands, a square of linen, a ring, a small rock, a Cathar Bible, a poem. When I leave, I will take them with me so they won't be forgotten, so that all traces of the believers won't be erased from this earth. Some tell me where their own treasures are buried— money, plate, gold and silver—all waiting for a time when the carnage will end. A time I know will never come."

"Amidée, my darling girl, looks up at me with large, hopeful eyes. 'Remember me' she says, as she carefully places her only prize in my hands. An arm's length of frayed twine is all that I have to remember that she lived.

"Women are softly crying, the crusaders' camp thunders below, and a baby wails to be nursed. There is not much time. It is urgent that I leave now.

"The other three are waiting, and I have no time for one last goodbye to Durand. Doat is there, and he stops what he is doing as I arrive, then wipes his runny nose on his sleeve as he stares. My heart stops. He is to be one of our four. There are two other men. Rene, a blacksmith, will be the leader, Peyre and myself. Each of us carries a leather pack.

"A barrage of stones comes raining down near where I am standing, and I quickly flatten myself against the wall for protection. Only moments later I hear the screams of the unlucky people below. My eyes water against the gust of cold wind carrying smoke from the burning fires, and even the chilly March winds cannot mask the smell of death and decay. It's time to leave.

"In pitch dark, I pick my way with the others across the cliff's narrow path and hug the slate surface as I inch along. Below me, the night's darkness envelopes my descent into the forested abyss. Up and to the left a faint glow from the soldier's camps lights up the west corner in the night's dim light. Noise from the camp's horses mingles with moaning from the sick and dying at Montségur.

"I am sweating and can hear the others as they strain their muscles. A piece of rubble is knocked off the cliff and I hold my breath as the rocks bounce off the debris below. Even in the dark, I can feel everyone stiffen and wait the unbearable few minutes until it is safe to continue.

"At long last, I can feel branches by my feet, but I know that I am still double my length before touching ground. Descending at a painfully slow pace, I stretch my foot out hoping to feel something solid and am finally rewarded by the soft earth of the Lasset Gorge. My arms ache at having tensed my muscles for so long. My knees give away; my legs tremble. I have made it, but there is no time for me to recover. Rene whispers for me to follow his voice and come quickly. I must force my shaking legs to move.

"After some time, we arrive at a cave, and one by one stoop to climb inside the opening of a large cavern. As we light our tapers, our dark sanctuary brightens. Almost in unison we let out a gasp, for as we look up we behold a glorious sight, one I had seen before when my father became a Perfect. The ceiling of the cave is painted in a familiar dark blue with hundreds of golden stars everywhere. Lit only by our candles, it looks as if the roof is transparent and the night sky itself is shining through. This holy place reminds me of a kinder time and I am lulled into feeling secure.

"Though the entrance is well hidden by brush and forest, our tapers are extinguished. In hushed voices, we reconfirm our next steps in the blackness of our sanctuary. Each of us is to go in a different direction and to remain in designated cities until the packages we each carry can be recovered by the next keepers.

"As the only female in the group I am to make my way to Montaillou where I will stay with a Catholic family sympathetic to our cause. From there, I will head to Carcassonne where I will find a safe house with a merchant. The others have their own destinations. Like me, none of us know exactly what we carry, only that it must be safely hidden and protected with our lives.

The plan is to rest until daybreak; then we'll separate, taking alternative paths through the forests. Doat suggests that he take first watch. Exhausted from the climb and eager to sleep, the rest of us agree."

A sudden pain in India's chest made her lurch forward and clutch at her heart. Squeezing her eyes tight, she breathed through the pain. Not yet. Please, not yet. After several anxious minutes, the pain subsided. When she opened her eyes, it was to Jourdain's worried face, his hand on hers.

"India, are you all right? Can you hear me?"

She coughed and fluttered her hand. "Better now. Perhaps I should try to remember more from a distance."

"Perhaps this is enough for today."

"No. Please, please let me finish. Favia may be back soon. It's important you know everything. Where was I? Ah, yes. In the cave, I awoke to someone sharply grabbing my arm. When I turned, I found myself looking directly into those lifeless gray eyes of Doat. He roughly pulled me to my feet, his bulk and size leaving me no choice but to be pushed in whichever direction he chose. Although in pain, I attempted to kick my way to freedom. I was angry and demanded that he let me go. For that, I received a backhand that sent me flying into the wall. As I held my flaming cheek in my hand, I smelled the familiar metallic odor of blood. I turned my head, and in the dim light I could make out the slit throats of my companions."

"My God, what have you done?" I screamed.

"Nothing I haven't been paid well to do. Now I'm going to show you what my private sword can do before you join your heretic friends." The lust in his eyes was terrifying.

"In one quick stride, he easily grabbed my arm with one hand while the other roughly groped my tender breasts. I was so angry that I was crying. He fumbled with my bodice while the stench from his fetid panting made me want to vomit. His hands were everywhere ripping, grabbing, hurting, and I begged him to stop. "Please don't, I'm with child.""

"What's this? The Templar's stuck you with child, did he?" With that, he slammed his pelvis into me with a force that took my breath away. I could feel his hardness against me, and every fiber of my being intensified into rage. I would not be violated.

"In that moment I felt the warrior rise from deep within me. My anger became focused, my nails dug into anything, his face, his arm. He slapped me hard again, and I fell backwards. Momentarily stunned, but as he came toward me my eye caught sight of the dagger by his side. Without even thinking, I grabbed it, plunged deeply and sliced across."

"In a flash it was over. His eyes were wide, glazed in pain and filled with the comprehension that he was about to die. It was obvious that he couldn't breathe, for he gasped for air as I fell against the cave wall. Stumbling forward a step, he fell and did not move. For what felt like ages, I just stared at his body as he lay dead in a pool of blood at my feet, the hem of my pants soaking up the thickening gore. Although I had killed before, Doat's betrayal shook me to my core.

The cave was no longer safe; it had been tainted with murder. I gathered everyone's bags and feeling the weight of my precious charge through the heavy sacking, I concentrated only on the task before me. Through a situation not of my choosing, I had become the keeper of the entire Cathar treasure."

Exhausted, India stopped, her head falling back onto her chair. She took a minute before speaking.

"I have waited and watched all these years for another initiate to come, but I see now the grail chooses its own. I need to rest, my son. Reliving these memories has tired me out. I know you have questions but hold them for just one more day. There is more to explain. The treasure's secrets are extremely powerful and hold grave danger to the uninitiated."

"I am without voice, but yes, I have many, many questions," Jourdain replied. "But it is obvious that you need to rest. All this talk has made you exhausted and to continue would be foolhardy. Let me help you to your bed. We can continue when you feel better."

Arm in arm, heads lowered to better secure their footing, and each deep in thought, they slowly shuffled towards the open door. As they reached the hallway, they both looked up and gasped, for through the darkness it was Favia's sharp eyes that smiled back.

Chapter Eighteen

Grabbing India's arm, Favia turned to Jourdain and smiled, but there was no compassion in her actions. "I'll take over now."

"That's kind of you, but we'll manage."

"Sir, you are barely out of bed yourself, and it will not do if either of you fall. It's best that I take her, and you rest yourself. Is that not right, India?"

India took a quick look at Jourdain. "Yes, of course, that makes good sense." She patted his arm. "And bless you for your patience with my crazy ramblings."

"Not at all, Madame. If you will excuse me, I'll go rest as you suggest."

Both Favia and India watched him slowly maneuver his way through the dark passage towards his room. Before he turned the corner, he took one last look at India, and then disappeared into the darkness.

India was weak. Favia could tell by her pallid complexion and shortness of breath, her steps slow and fearful. So she was surprised when India suddenly stopped, squeezed her arm and stared hard into her eyes.

"What did you hear?"

"I heard nothing. I had only just returned and came to check on you as I always do."

"I don't believe you."

"Believe whatever you want. I heard you say you were tired and I came to help. Isn't that what you pay me for?"

"I pay you to mind your own business. Just take me to my room, then, ensure our guest gets something to eat."

"Bien sûr Madame, of course."

In truth, Favia's mind was racing with the possibilities of her newfound information. Should she tell Prades everything? Should she wait to listen for more? The question was, which way made her the most money? If she played along that she had heard nothing, she'd know where the treasure was hidden next time they talked, but then what would be done about Jourdain? What if he left with the information or took it himself? She needed Jourdain out of the picture, preferably before he heard anything more. Favia's heart started to race, pieces of her plan fitting together faster than she could think. If she could get Jourdain to leave and the "real" keeper were to show up, India would be forced to confess.

She was thinking of this when she brought a large bowl of pottage to Jourdain. He was standing by the window, obviously deep in thought, for he didn't react when she entered the room.

"Your dinner, Monsieur."

"Merci. Just leave it over there."

"May I speak openly with you?"

"Of course."

"I overheard some of what India was telling you."

Jourdain spun around to look at her. "And what exactly do you think you heard?"

"Enough to know heresy when I hear it."

"She's an old woman who has done me a kindness, and I am simply repaying her by listening to foolishness."

"Perhaps, but these are dangerous times, and I'm sure you know what the cost would be if her 'foolishness' were to be reported to the authorities. I may be just a servant, but I would think that a confidante to heresy would be just as heavily implicated, and we certainly know where that leads. If I were you, I'd go home to my wife and son. I guarantee there is nothing here for you but trouble."

"That sounds like a threat."

"Not at all. I happen to know that India's activities have interested certain parties so consider it just a friendly warning lest you decide to extend your stay."

"If you're so worried about heresy, why do you stay?"

"Because despite what she says, I have been with her so long that she's like a mother to me. Really, the only mother I've ever known. Who would protect her or care for her if I left?"

In the moment of silence that followed, she eyed him as he obviously evaluated her words. Despite his bravado, there was fear in his eyes.

"I appreciate your concern, but your warning is unnecessary. I was already making plans to leave." The fear tainted his words as well.

"I'm sure your family will be very happy to see you, Monsieur, so well recovered from your injuries and alive. Let me know if there's anything I can do to help with your journey. Excuse me. I have other chores to take care of."

Favia couldn't believe her luck, and how easily he was intimidated. Everything was falling together. After her chores, she'd send word to Prades that they needed to meet. Better yet, she'd go there herself. In the meantime, though, she'd start to scan every crack, niche and corner of the house. If the treasure was hidden here, she'd find it. Then she'd bargain.

* * * *

India felt sick to her stomach. Although Favia acted as though she had heard nothing of their conversation, she didn't believe a word of it, and she didn't trust the girl. There was only one thing to do and no more time to wait.

Slowly, and with great difficulty, she rose from her bed, trying to ignore, or at least wince, through her aching muscles and the pain in her arthritic knees. In an attempt to shuffle as quietly as she could, it took forever just to reach the other side of the room to her writing table and chair. It took even longer for her to catch her breath. She looked down and sadly realized this would be her last opportunity to tell Jourdain everything he needed to know. With her time running out, she picked up her quill and prepared herself to write into the long wee hours of the night.

* * * *

Jourdain gingerly unwrapped the bandage from around his arm and tested his agility by moving his appendage back and forth several times.

111

It was sore, but he'd be able to handle a horse well enough if he rested enroute. Whoever India was, she was an excellent healer, he'd grant her that. It was clear that Favia had heard everything and that placed him in a very precarious position. He was obviously right to not trust her. India had promised him gold, but what use would that be if he were burned as a heretic? What use would riches be if his family was branded along with him? He owed Maura and Leo his protection and silently prayed that if he could just return home safely he would never question his faith again. He'd hate to refuse India, for there was something about her that tugged at his heartstrings. There was such power in that aged little body. But he was in over his head. Mother, benefactress, treasure keeper or crazy woman, he wanted none of it. He'd gather his things together and leave at first light.

* * * *

Favia slid out into the darkness of the damp city street. Misty droplets speckled her shawl as she wrapped it tightly around her head and shoulders. Wary of her reckless decision to walk the streets alone, she kept a good lookout for thieves and drunks. Dark city streets were never a good choice for a lone female, but she needed to speak with Prades tonight.

A thin, disembodied arm reached out of a dark doorway and pawed at the air near her shoulder. A drunken women's shrill voice called to her from the black recess.

"A sous for some wine?"

Favia scurried out of reach and shivered as the drunk's cackling trailed behind her through the filthy streets.

All the way there, she rehearsed what she would say. Her plan was perfect, brilliant even. In fact, she'd insist that he return her home by carriage, coins in her pocket.

Her knock on the door yielded a tall, thin servant, dressed in quality cloth and a sneer that assured her that M. del Cros could want nothing from the likes of her. She, however, would not be dissuaded. Raising herself to her full height, she imagined herself to be a woman of quality. "I demand to speak with your master on an item of utmost importance, and should you not fetch him immediately you will only have yourself to blame for M. del Cros's anger."

"Wait here," he retorted as he shut the door in her face.

After several minutes, the door was reopened. The same dour face steeled his eyes in her direction.

"Apparently, my Master will see you," he spat out in distaste.

"Well, imagine that? Such prompt service for the likes of me." She strutted behind him through a long dark hallway, past several closed doorways, until they reached a large salon.

A blazing fire warmed the room, and it was prettily decorated in worn silks of soft blues and rose. Prades was sitting on a long settee, a drink in his hand, talking to another man who stood near the hearth.

The other man was tall and thin and dressed in the dark shades of the clergy. His prominent nose dominated his face and was no doubt raised for full effect. He was obviously in mid-sentence when she arrived, for his thin mouth froze and he immediately stopped talking. Small black beady eyes pierced through her as if to question her audacity to interrupt him, and in that instant she panicked. Prades glanced her way.

"Favia, to what do I owe this unexpected visit? Did the cloth not arrive as arranged?"

"No, it arrived well enough, thank you. It's just that I've come on the other matter."

"The other matter, you say. Well then, your visit is indeed fortuitous, for let me introduce my friend, Renier de Beynac. Renier, this is the young lady I was speaking to you about."

"A pleasure to meet you, Mademoiselle." Renier walked over to where she stood and looked her, a look of both disgust and amusement in his eyes. "I am guessing you have information that couldn't wait until morning? But then you are probably used to traveling the streets at night, non?"

"Yes, sir, I mean no, sir. I mean I felt the information was important enough for me to put my safety at risk to ensure M. del Cros received it."

"Indeed. Well, do not let me interfere with this important information. Come on then, out with it, girl."

Confused, Favia looked to Prades for reassurance. Who was this man?

"Forgive me, but are you sure you want me to discuss the other matter in front of this gentleman?"

At that, Renier burst out in a loud guffaw, spewing out wine through coughs as his head shook. "Oh, this is rich. Really, Prades, the little wench is besotted with you. What have you promised her? Out with it, girl. I am not a patient man, and as you seem unaware, I will inform you that any dispersal of funds that go in your direction come directly from me. I will be the judge of the quality of your information, so I suggest that you start talking now. Save your cow eyes for Prades later."

Favia understood him clearly, and Prades' cough and slight nod confirmed it. He was the man with the money, and if she wanted any, she'd better make it worth his while.

"I have heard with my own ears, sir, my mistress, India Serras, admit that she is a heretic and participated in the resistance at Montségur. Furthermore, she said she is the keeper of the entire Cathar treasure and seems to think that an injured man we took in is the next keeper. She means to tell him where it is, but I've taken care of him. And I have a plan."

Prades snapped his head in her direction. "You've murdered him?"

"No, of course not. I merely suggested his life and that of his family's might be in danger should he be implicated with India. He's leaving tomorrow."

Renier turned to Prades. "An interesting young woman you've recruited, del Cros."

"I'm beginning to notice that."

"And your plan?"

"Well, for as long as I've been there, the only thing that India ever does is to sit and watch out her window. I've always thought that it was because she's a nosy old snoop, but yesterday I heard her tell this Jourdain that she's been watching for this 'keeper' person for years. I think that because he's the only person to show up on her doorstep she thinks it must be him. Now if he was gone and one of you were to claim to be the real keeper, she'd have to tell you, wouldn't she?"

Renier simply stared at her and slowly clapped his hands. "Prades, I would say Favia has earned herself a few coins, do you not agree?"

"I do, indeed."

"And a carriage ride home to ensure my safety?"

Renier smiled and slowly, purposely, strode to her side. "The safety of your soul and your person is my prime concern. Prades, escort the young lady to her carriage, will you? You can expect me within the next two days ...and Favia?"

"Yes?"

In a flash, he snapped his hand around her fragile neck. "You'll be a good girl and say nothing to anyone, won't you?"

She looked into his black, soulless eyes and quickly nodded.

Chapter Nineteen

The night was long, hot and sticky which only added to Jourdain's discomfort. He was already tossing and turning over his decision to leave. There was no question that it was the prudent thing to do, but he wrestled with his conscience at leaving India to Favia and the possibility of a heretic's inquisition. There was no way he could take her with him. Even if she did survive the journey, Maura wouldn't stand for it, and it would be only a matter of time before she'd realize India's religious leanings. Besides that, there was no way he would place his own family in danger.

If he could leave without getting any further involved, without any danger to himself, leave with his horse and enough food to get himself home, he'd gladly go to as many masses as Maura wanted. He just wanted to go home. He just wanted to wake up from this nightmare and pretend none of it ever happened.

He thought back to his conversations with India over the past few days. Maybe she was just a crazy old woman. Maybe none of what she said ever happened. Could she really be his mother? Yes. It was no secret that he had been given to a childless older couple, but he knew nothing more than that. An unusual birthmark didn't prove anything.

What he couldn't deny was the connection he felt to her. It was beyond gratitude, beyond promises. It was something more, like a bond, a recognition from his soul. He genuinely liked her, wanted to take care of her. No matter how crazy her story sounded, he had only to think back to her quivering voice, her tears, the intensity of how she looked at him, to know her words were truth, at least to her. Anyone else in his position wouldn't hesitate to leave, yet he wrestled with the thought of abandoning her. What in God's name was he supposed to do?

His hands cradled his bowed head, and he thought about his friend Alfreid—his smile, his jokes, and he winced as he swallowed a lump at the memory of his last sight of him. India had made inquiries and then, at her own expense, had had his body returned to his family. She had done this without question or complaint. Rubbing his scalp, he closed his eyes and let out a long sigh. He stared at the wall and wished that he knew how to pray. If ever there was a time where he needed an answer, or Divine intervention, it was now.

Dear God, tell me what to do. Get me out of this. Let me go home. Just let me go home.

It was the touch on his arm that woke him up. It was still dark, his room silent, filled with the stillness of shadows. He turned his head towards the sound of a slight movement and held his breath. The dark shape by his bedside was the only indication that he was not alone, and a heightened sense of fear made him jump.

"Who's there?"

"Jourdain, be still. It's me, India."

"India? Is everything all right? Are you okay? You scared me in the dark like that. It's not yet dawn."

"I am aware of that, but you must hear what I have to say. You must leave, and you must leave now."

Swinging his bare feet to the floor from his cot, he looked towards her voice, and then rubbed his forehead. Reaching for his chemise, he briefly registered the freshly laundered smell, then stopped.

"What did you just say?"

India moved closer and grasped his hand. "You have to leave. Now."

"In God's name, tell me what's happened?"

"This is more about what will happen soon. Everything is unfolding as it was prophesied, and for the second time in your life, Jourdain, you leaving me is the only way to ensure your safety and survival as well as the treasure."

"And what of your safety and survival? Surely you know that you cannot trust Favia."

"Of course, I know this. That's why I did not light a taper and we are speaking in whispers, in the dark, in my own home. Look, we don't have much time. Favia is sleeping, but she'll be up soon enough. I have things to say and something of utmost importance to give you. I ask only that you keep what I give you safe. Once you have returned home, read what I have written in privacy. All will be explained. If I leave you one piece of advice, then I leave you this. There is not a soul that you can share this with, for there is power in what you now must guard.

"There is no time to explain everything in detail, but there is a cup in the several items that I will give you. This cup is ordinary looking, dirty, scuffed; in fact, it will seem to be anything but of its true nature. Do not let it fool you. Keep it wrapped and do not touch it in any way."

"What?"

"Hear me out, for this is not an item to be trifled with. The greatest of what you guard is the grail, and it is an object not entirely of earthly matter. It is a thing of both the world of physical and spirit, but belongs to neither. The cup has remarkable abilities and presents itself differently to whoever gazes upon it. To even hold it for a short time is enough to considerably extend one's lifetime."

"You?"

"Surely you have wondered at my own longevity? It is rumored that it can even raise the dead, although it's beyond me why anyone would want to come back."

"Tell me the truth. Do you speak of devilry, or do you speak of the grail, the Holy cup of Jesus?"

"The children of Jesus and Mary Magdalene were taken to France, where their blood descendants founded the Merovingian dynasty of the early kings of France. This cup, Jourdain, is of the Merovingian Kings and the sacred bloodline they carry. I cannot emphasize enough the power it holds. As I said before, the cup is neither spirit nor matter. It protects the one who guards it, yet reflects, and amplifies the soul of the one who uses it. A dark intent reflects a dark soul, does it not? It is a thing that must be guarded so that, in time, a spirit truly worthy of yielding its power will claim it.

"Were this the only treasure I pass on to you it would be enough to place your life in danger till the end of your days, but there is more. In the satchel, you will find a wooden book of names and lineages dating

118

back to Jesus and the Magdalene. There is another, thick and heavy, with documentation about many things, as well as the lost Gospel of Mary Magdalene. Protect them with your life. I have no more time to explain things to you, but I've written as much as I can, as much as I know.

"Many years ago I had to make a difficult decision, to stay or to go, to live or to die. It was one of the hardest decisions I have ever had to make, but had I not chosen to accept my task, we would not be here talking. I did what I needed to do, and now it is your turn to do what you must."

"India. I beg of you to choose someone else to guard these items. I am a simple man of simple worth. I am no knight. I am no brave Templar who yields a sword."

"Listen to me. You don't know half of who you are and the blood that runs through your veins. Your future is clear and etched deeply into the records. I've read it for myself. Listen well to my words, for it is no accident that we have met. From this point onwards, you must choose the path of higher purpose and never falter from it, for a much greater task awaits you. Do you understand?"

"Yes. I still want to believe that this is all just craziness, but yes, yes, I understand."

"Then promise me that you will do exactly what I ask."

"I promise."

For several minutes, they sat in dark silence until Jourdain felt himself enfolded into an awkward stiff hug.

"It's time to go, my son."

* * * *

Jourdain found himself riding outside the city gates just as the sun's rays peeked over the horizon. His side hurt from the rocking movements of his horse, but he didn't mind. He was going home. She had everything arranged, packed and had given him coin and food. He simply had to make the decision to leave, and after all, it was what he had wanted. Maybe God had heard his prayers. The cloudless sky promised a day of warmth and respite from a world of fear, and after so long being indoors, he drank in the beauty of the morning. The hills filled his lungs and soul with the fresh morning air and renewed hope. He was safe.

As he slowly rode on, the road became dotted with merchants on their way towards the city with wagons laden high with vegetables and goods for sale, their heads nodding in acknowledgement as he passed them by. He smiled. Only weeks ago that had been him.

His life had changed. He could sense that something about him was different. How could he return home now and pretend that everything was the same? It wasn't. He'd have to lie for rest of his life, for he certainly couldn't tell anyone about India, let alone her tale.

Was it possible for him to just bury the satchel she had given him and carry on with his life? Maybe. In fact, he thought that idea had merit to it. He weighed those words for some time as his horse plodded on until he began to see the wisdom in them. That would be fulfilling his promise to her and at the same time keep himself and his family safe. The question was where? If he brought it home, Maura would find it. That much was certain. He would need a place somewhere remote, a location where it would be safe from thieves and the elements. His travels had really only taken him along safe roads to and from cities and nothing came to mind.

He worried about what would happen to India. Although he carried whatever physical evidence might incriminate her, she would know no safety. It took only words and suspicion for the Inquisition to take notice, and Favia had that. There was no doubt that she had heard enough to know there was something of value for the taking.

India, however, was her sole source of food and lodging, and without a treasure, he doubted she would risk losing that. Really, at worst, she would probably spend her days going through every nook and cranny in that house trying to find it. The more he thought about it, the more he felt satisfied that he need not do anything more than hide the satchel and return home. The question, though, was still where?

These thoughts kept him occupied, oblivious to food or pain, until late afternoon when he passed an inn with aromas of roasted meats that practically swept him off his horse. India had graciously given him a large purse of coin. Odd, because Favia said she had none. She had appeared to be a frugal old widow.

He toyed with the idea of stopping at the inn for the night instead of carrying on till dusk at the next inn. He was hot and tired and his arm ached. He would stay here for the night, read her letter and then hide it along with the rest of the items in his satchel before returning home. As a servant stepped out from the door holding a large freshly-baked pannier, he was engulfed by aromas that made his head spin and stomach growl. The decision was made. He secured his horse with the stable boy and gingerly shouldered his packs inside, careful not to strain his injured arm. It took only moments to order a hot plate of stew and a cold beer, the best he had tasted in months. All he needed now was a clean bed in a room where he could be alone with his thoughts. Within minutes of showing enough coin, he found himself on a comfortable cot in a room that contained a window and a small table. The window he needed for light. It was already late afternoon and he needed as much natural light as possible to read all that she had written.

There were two satchels, one larger than the other, and he eyed them both. It was the latter that he grabbed first in the assumption that it carried the treasure. Instead he pulled out hard biscuits, several dried poultices for his arm, a second chemise, a loaf of bread, a dagger and another large purse filled with coin. He grabbed the second, took a deep breath and looked inside. Tucked away into the dark leather satchel were five items individually wrapped in soft white silk. Two looked like books, the third was a square box about the size of a man's fist, the fourth seemed to hold several sheets of vellum, and the fifth was an object with an odd square-like shape. The fourth package he opened first and slowly laid out seven sheets of the finest vellum before him on the bed.

Her writing was spindly, at times thin, at others bold, but all together, side-by-side like that, there was a beautiful movement to her words, as if she had written a river that ebbed and flowed from page to page. Taking the first one, he began to read.

* * * *

Prades had to credit Favia. For a mere servant girl, she was brilliant. It was she who suggested that Jourdain be followed just in case, and she was right. How else would the man have afforded the inn, let alone the bags he carried? All Prades knew was that if there was treasure in those satchels, it would be his. Favia would be easy enough to dispose of later.

121

As for Renier, what he didn't know existed, Prades didn't need to share. He found the proprietor as he sat at a table of men stroking the end of his nose. He was a shifty, thin man with an all but bald pate, and he didn't need reasons.

Throwing down more than enough coin, Prades simply demanded, "I'll take the room next to the gentleman in the single."

The innkeeper gave him one quick look. "As you wish, Monsieur."

One swipe and the coins were gone.

Chapter Twenty

Mémoires de India Serras

My dearest Son,

There is much that you know, but so much more to say that I hardly know where to begin. If you are reading this, then you will have already noticed the other linen-wrapped items in the satchel. It is imperative that you read my words first, before opening anything, and to follow all my instructions in this letter. Commit my words to memory and then destroy them all.

What you carry in these bags is not what you think. The night you arrived, I had all but given up hope and had begun to write my memoirs. I have included these pages for you, as they hold important information you will need to find where the real treasure has been hidden. Have no doubt, though, that what you carry is most dangerous, and what you are perceived to be carrying could cost you your life.

Amongst these notes, you will find two legal documents. One is my last will and testament with a detailed list of my linen, plate and silver. The other is the deed to my house in Carcassonne, for I leave everything to you. I have also left directions for where my family's trunk was buried so very long ago. These are for you to do with what you will. They are material things only. Keep them, give them away, or sell them if you want. They mean nothing to me.

In the same satchel, you will find what I truly value. It is the odd-shaped object wrapped with a piece of string that, itself, is very dear to me. Like the others, it is wrapped in linen, but look closely underneath, and you will find a symbol, a tiny red cross-patois embroidered on the corner. I leave you a strong word of warning to touch nothing that does not have this mark. Look closely at it. I assume you will recognize it, for it is a copy of the birthmark you bare on your left shoulder.

It is of this birthmark that I speak of next. It is important, Jourdain, that you understand the blood that runs through your veins. Your father bore the same mark, as did his father, and his father before him.

The symbol of this birthmark is known as the cross patois whose roots begin way before the time of Christ. My son, your lineage is a long and distinguished one dating back to Merovingian Kings who all bore this mark. It is this that distinguishes them from all other men and renders them immediately identifiable to higher initiates. That is why there can be no mistaking who you are. It is no surprise that the grail has chosen you, for it was my grandfather, and then your father, who was the grail's guardian before you. The promise I made to keep it safe was to him.

Lastly, know this. I die gladly now with my heart at ease, for I have been blessed with having had you, even briefly, in my life.

Be safe and know that as the rightful sacred keeper of all that is held secret, you are guided and protected by a power higher than anything on this earth.

Je t'aime, mon fils.

India

Jourdain tilted his head back and squinted. Rationally, he questioned her words, yet he felt proud, stronger, as if a long silent strength inside him had been awakened by the knowledge that his bloodline was from ancient kings. As for the birthmark, it was as she had said. It did indeed clearly resemble a red cross, something Maura interpreted as giving him protection from evil.

Looking at the other sheets, he picked up what was obviously India's will. Why would she do this for a stranger unless she really believed him to be her son? Gently placing it beside the first, he reached for another longer narrative.

Mémoires de India Serras

Branches scratched at my face leaving traces of welts. My hands were cold and the dampness bit into me, but there was no opportunity to stop and get warm. I had to keep on moving. Onward I fled through the dense brush, stopping only to catch my breath and to listen for footsteps of anyone who might be following me. For four days, I travelled only in the early hours and at dusk when it was safe to do so. Muck and dead leaves clung to my wooden clogs oozing the frigid water into my already wet feet. Branches slapped at my face as I ran. Not daring to light a fire in case it attracted attention, I ate only dry bread washed down with water from a stream.

I prayed that the cloak of darkness would hide my movements from those who would do me harm. I wanted nothing more than to be with Durand, no longer a part of this physical earth, no longer a part of this madness. I barely slept; the days became a haze of running, hiding. I moved constantly, looking for safe places to spend the night. After four days of heading in a northwest direction, I happened across an old ruined Roman well and stopped to catch my breath. Overgrown with vines and weeds, the stones were crumbling and worn. The pool, empty from a long dried-up spring, was dusty and filled with dead leaves, sticks and crumbling mortar. I surveyed my surroundings, which were still in thick forestland. To my right, there was a large embankment with stony outcrops, while to my left, about ten paces away, I could hear the babbling of a small brook. Walking over to the water, I dipped my rough hands in to scoop up a drink. The water was icy cold and my fingers immediately ached at the chill. It was what I needed, though, and I drank my fill and felt refreshed.

Finding a sizable rock towards the embankment to lean against, I collapsed and decided to rest my weary body. I checked my pack beside me and fingered the leather wrappings protecting my sacred packages. How desperately I wanted a warm fire, a hot meal, Durand's gentle touch. An inconsolable pain stabbed my heart. When would this end?

As I looked up towards the rocks, I saw something that I had not noticed before. Hidden behind a tangle of hedges was a small opening that looked like a cave, cleverly hidden. I climbed up to investigate. Although cold and growing dark, the cave was somewhat hospitable. The charred remains of old logs gave mute acknowledgement that someone long ago had also sought shelter here, perhaps even other Cathars.

The cave seemed to extend for some distance, but I was reluctant to explore any farther than the entrance, at least not without a torch.

I dropped my sack. The first order would be to light a small fire. The thought of warmth brought a smile to my face as I looked around for dry wood. I was surprised to see another small pile of dried faggots tucked neatly away behind a boulder. The cave had obviously been uninhabited for years, but I still looked around for any further signs of life. Finding none, I relaxed somewhat and gathered up the wood.

I unpacked my tinderbox and soon had a small fire going. Placing my hands and feet close to its warmth, I allowed myself to absorb all that had happened and began to cry so hard that I feared I could not stop.

Hearing a rustling in the bushes, I spun around, ready to run or fight, but it was only a stray dog walking slowly towards me. He was obviously hungry, and his ribs showed through his mangy coat. His head lowered and ears alerted to my tone, I coaxed the animal closer while breaking off a piece of my stale bread. I tossed the chunk to him and was amused as he swallowed it mid-air. I then tossed him another and the animal moved closer, no longer wary, his tail slowly wagging. Nuzzling his nose into my palm, he quietly lay beside me as if we had been longtime friends. I called him Ami.

As the stars blanketed the night sky, I spread my cloak over a cushion of pine needles, closed my eyes and let a soft wind high in the pines whisper me to sleep.

I stayed in this cave four more days feeling safer than I had in years. During those days, I had time to reflect quietly and to explore what had become my sanctuary. The back of the cave split slightly to the right, and towards the back of this passage were several layers of naturally occurring shelves. The shelves themselves extended even farther into the walls of the cave and provided an excellent place to hide much of what I carried. I spent my last day ensuring that everything, including the cave, stayed well hidden.

It took me another two days of walking due west to reach the home that had been arranged for me, and by this time my body had begun to thicken, confirming what I had already knew. You will know the couple well~a leather merchant and his wife, Rosemonde and Landri Le Tardif.

My time with your adoptive parents was a true gift of love, and I thank the stars above that Rosemonde was in my life. She was a true inspiration, and because of her, I think I became a gentler person and certainly a more compassionate one. Recognizing that I was with child, she insisted that I stay with them during my confinement. During that time, she encouraged my interest in herbal medicine, and many of my days were spent either dispensing ointments, teas and salves, or tending the garden of mint, echinacea, nettle and raspberry leaves for use in my compounds. It was a time of gentle healing for me, and in a short time, you were born.

My joy, however, was to be short-lived. The Inquisition continued to hunt for Cathar stragglers, and I was terrified of what the future would bring. Would you, too, be thrown into a burning pyre? The thought of me dying had just become a matter of consequence, but the thought of anyone harming my child was more than I could bear. I did the only thing I could, and it was to give you to them for safekeeping. Ami, the dog, who had become my companion, stayed as well. I liked to think that he guarded you well.

I returned to my cave again before traveling here to Carcassonne to ensure everything remained safely hidden and to paint the ceiling in the fashion of another that I had seen. I also marked the entrance with a certain symbol you will no doubt recognize.

Jourdain blinked. 'Ami' was indeed the dog he grew up with, and Rosemonde and Landri were his adoptive parents. He sat there with the paper in his hands for a few minutes just staring at the wall. Everything that she had said was the truth.

Looking inside the bag, he took out one of the book-shaped items and turned it over. There was the embroidered mark, just as she had said. Gently unfolding the linen, he found an ancient tome in blackened leather. On the front, stamped in gold that was cracked and flaking from age, was a triangle and the letters 'Ignis,' the Latin word for fire. As he opened the aged cover, a waft of must and mold assaulted his nose and he resisted an urge to sneeze.

Turning the first page, he read, "To move into the energy of fire is to be utterly consumed, transformed and lifted out of limitation. Fire represents divine energy, purification, revelation, and transformation. To purposely transform an earthly body into the soul's divine spark through this ancient alchemical symbol is known as a perfect fire."

Wrapping it back up, he replaced the book and pulled out the box-shaped item. It felt heavy, but didn't have the symbol, and he quickly put it back without opening it.

He then pulled out the odd-shaped object and quickly found the symbol. When he opened it slowly, a number of items tumbled onto the bed: a small piece of red velvet, a hair comb, a square of linen, a ring, a small rock, a Cathar Bible, a poem and an arm's length of frayed twine. He thought back to her words only spoken the other day. These were the items given to her before she escaped. These were the items she treasured above all else for they reminded her of people with hopes and dreams and families.

The light dimmed, and his eyes grew heavy with the strain of having expended so much physical effort combined with a long day of riding. He let out a long low sigh and replaced the objects in the satchel. He knew now what he must do and would leave at first light.

* * * *

Del Cros was awakened early by movement in the next room. It was not yet first light, and he was irritated at the thought of rising much earlier than he usually did. The early morning air was heavy and damp, and the yard was shrouded in a thick blanket of fog. With some difficulty, he quietly followed Jourdain as he collected his horse and secured the packs. Realizing that in the fog he could easily lose sight of him, Del Cros walked into the stable and nodded a greeting to the stable boy. Although he got a good look at Jourdain's face, the man barely noticed his because he was so intent on securing the two satchels he carried.

Expecting Jourdain to head in the same direction he took yesterday, he was alarmed to see him turn back towards Carcassonne. He could not allow Jourdain to return, so he quickly formulated a new plan. His intent would no longer be just a theft. Feeling for his dagger, he booted his horse into a gallop down an alternative path that would suit his needs nicely.

* * * *

The reverberation from the horse's hooves echoed through the mists making a sound that was eerie and surreal. Blanketed by the fog, Jourdain felt as if he were in another world and fearfully looked around lest thieves be waiting. The fog reminded him of recent events, and he fingered the hilt of the dagger that he carried by his side. Ahead, and off to the right, he could barely ascertain the distant shadowy peaks from the nearby chateau he had passed yesterday. The road was sculpted with muddy wagon tracks dried and caked into ruts that caused his horse to misstep as he plodded along. He calculated that it would be late by the time he arrived. He only hoped that he would arrive in time. Irritated that he had not thought of this sooner, he pictured the money purse that India had safely tucked away in the satchel. The amount was more than enough to buy the silence of a greedy servant girl.

The road continued to wind through a meadow heavily shrouded with the morning's mist, and as his horse passed by a small copse, a lone horseman stepped into his path. His heart pounded and pulse quickened until he realized that it was only the man he had seen this morning at the inn.

"Good morning, friend," he greeted.

"Good morning. I'm sorry to startle you, but I recognized you from the inn and saw that we were headed in the same direction. Carcassonne, non?"

"Oui."

"Good. We can travel together, then. Have you broken fast? I have plenty of food to share, and if you like, we can stop here. No one is around, and I assure you, you are quite safe with me," the stranger declared.

Jourdain, relaxed. In fact, he'd welcome some company on this trip.

"To whom do I owe a thanks?"

"Prades del Cros, and no thanks is needed. I'm happy for the company to be honest with you." Dismounting from his horse, the man walked the animal over to a stand of young poplars and tied the reins to a lower branch. "And you are?"

"Jourdain Le Tardif." He walked his horse closer, dismounted and did the same. "I appreciate the company as well. I met up with some bad sorts several weeks ago. Lost a good friend because of it and had a close call myself." He patted his upper arm to suggest a wound but did not elaborate any further.

"What takes you to Carcassonne?"

"Family matters. My aging mother needs my help."

Del Cros, who had been pulling out a loaf of bread, fumbled with it, then quickly rescued it from the soil by brushing off the crust. "Your mother?"

"Yes, she's ill. And you?"

"My family has lived there for six generations. Chateau del Cros is my family home."

Jourdain looked at the man with new eyes. From the look of his shabby cloak, he wouldn't have guessed. He nodded an acknowledgement to his social standing. "A nobleman."

"Yes." Looking down at his clothes, the man shrugged. "Traveling attire only. It's never wise to dress too fine for the road."

They both found relatively dry places to sit with their backs resting against a couple of large boulders. Jourdain looked around. His view of his surroundings was limited due to the fog, but the small outcrop seemed to provide enough shelter and safety from wandering thieves. He tried to relax, but he could not shake the feeling that something was wrong.

"I'm honored for the company, then."

Del Cros gave him a long look and winked. "I wouldn't be if I were you."

Jourdain laughed, but his face blanched as the man seemed to make a point of slowly drawing out his dagger. The nobleman stared at him before letting out a loud guffaw. With a large, toothy grin, he drew the knife across the large wedge of softly ripened cheese he had pulled out and proceeded to smear the piece on chunks of bread before offering one to Jourdain.

Growing nervous about the man's dramatics, Jourdain managed a small smile and nodded his appreciation with a full mouth. Del Cros just chewed and stared. The two of them continued to eat in hungry silence, but every now and then the nobleman's mouth would curl into a smile, showing small, yellowed teeth and masticated bread.

"Your mother's ill?"

"Sort of. She's old, very frail and needs someone to take care of her."

"It sounds to me like you're making sure you get your fair share before she croaks."

"It's not like that at all. She has no money."

Prades looked up and stared hard. "If you say so."

Jourdain started to feel even more uncomfortable and shifted his weight against the rock he was leaning on. Although he appreciated the offer of food and companionship, his new acquaintance seemed a little odd.

To his left, a small bush sheltered an enormous spider's web coated in dewdrops that transformed the web into a necklace dripping with liquid jewels. A large, fat fly had become entangled, and he watched as the spider sat patiently for his prey to entrap himself farther. Feeling a little like the fly himself, Jourdain looked over to del Cros who still watched him closely, then grinned.

The mist had begun to lighten and rise dispelling into the cooled morning air. Jourdain took a deep breath and looked around for a place to relieve himself. Eyeing a bush a short distance away, he rose to his feet and began to loosen his belt.

"Many thanks for that. We should leave soon and get back on the road."

As he walked away, he gave a quick look back. Prades crossed his legs and began to clean under his nails with the point of his knife. As he looked up, he smiled again.

"Take your time."

Every fiber in his body felt alert, wary, yet except for this fellow's odd character, he had no reason to believe he should be in any danger. As he stood there relieving himself, he thought about India's words. "Have no doubt that what you are perceived to be carrying could cost you your life." A prickle of fear momentarily overwhelmed him, and he felt sick to his stomach. Quickly retying his belt, he strode back to the clearing and in that instant he knew he might not make it out alive. Del Cros stood there smiling, Jourdain's satchel in one hand and his dagger in the other.

"Well, well, the little wench was right."

"Put it down, Prades."

"You know, I doubted the little chit, but I figured I needed the money and why not? If I ended up in a better position, then it was worth the time, and I must say, Jourdain, you've definitely made it worth my time. Unfortunately, my friend, you'll have to die for it. Pity, because you seem to be decent enough."

"Favia."

"Of course. Favia told me and for very little incentive. As I recall, a quick tumble in the back alley sealed the deal."

"Look, you don't need to do this. Take it, take it all. Just leave me her letters and let me be on my way."

"You know, Jourdain, yesterday I would have happily agreed, but the circumstances have changed. You see, I've already read this first page and I can hardly wait to read the rest. I'm sure it's filled with lots of interesting secrets. You made the mistake, not me, my friend. After all, she did tell you to destroy her note, didn't she? I expect you'll be a bit of a disappointment to your mother with that lineage and all. Now you want to return to Carcassonne. Well, even you can see why I can't let you do that. I wouldn't mind seeing that special birthmark of yours, though. It matters not if you're dead or alive." Prades dropped the satchel, pointed the dagger towards Jourdain and took a long stride forward. "Things are about to get very messy."

Jourdain stood frozen and then mechanically moved his hand to his side and grasped the hilt of the small dagger he carried. Neither took their eyes off the other.

Prades smiled and circled around, waving his dagger from side to side like a viper ready to strike. With a thumping heart, Jourdain mimicked his opponent's moves and focused on his eyes. His injured side ached. His movements were slower, his skills weak, but his head was clear. He would have to kill del Cros or die.

Prades jutted forward, extending his dagger towards Jourdain's weak arm, but he turned just in time and the knife cut into fabric only. His heart pounded as they darted and circled, daggers poised for any opportunity for a killing strike. The tension thickened and sweat beaded their faces. Jourdain knew he was a mistake away from death and focused his attention on staying out of reach. Tiring del Cros out was his only strategy to evening out his odds.

"Face it, Jourdain, you're nothing but the bastard child of a heretic."

"Who are you to speak? You're no better that a common criminal."

"Really? Well, this criminal will see your mother's throat slit before she sees another sunrise. I can't have any loose ends, now can I?"

At that Jourdain stepped forward and in a blind fury slashed towards del Cros's side. A thin, bright crimson line bled through the man's shirt, and the look of surprise on his face bolstered Jourdain's determination.

"I'll grant you that little scratch, Jourdain, but you'll pay for it with your life."

The horses snorted and stomped in reaction to their agitated movements and caught Jourdain's attention. What he saw was an opportunity. Keeping Prades' back to the horses, he strategically circled and herded him towards a large oak near the tree to which the horses were tethered.

"Did you really think you could return to Carcassonne and save India? I'm doing you a favor. At least here, you're going to die like a man. Back there, Favia would have slit your throat while you slept. I'd be surprised if she hasn't killed India already."

"You're lying."

"Am I? Then kill me and find out for yourself."

Prades lunged and slashed at Jourdain's side. A warm sensation of liquid saturated his clothes and confirmed what he felt, a deep bloody gash. As he held his hand over his side, it quickly became bloodied. He would need to staunch the flow soon. He thought of Alfreid's face, dying in the city streets with his throat slashed. He thought of India alone and relying on him. He thought of his father, a Knight Templar, and the blood that coursed through his veins. He thought of his own son and vowed that he would walk away from this.

Without thought, strategy or warning, he held his dagger high and focused all his anger, frustrations and every last ounce of energy on his target and ran bellowing towards Prades at the top of his lungs. Taken aback by the unorthodox bull-like charge, Prades stumbled backwards and tripped on an exposed tree root. Falling against the oak, he dropped his dagger in the process. Wide-eyed with fear, the man watched as Jourdain was upon him in one giant stride, his knife against Prades' neck, as his voice raged with volume and intensity. In an instant, it was all over.

He was still screaming as the nobleman slumped to the ground, blood pooling around him, desperately fighting for his last gasps of air. Jourdain fell to the ground and sobbed.

Out of breath and exhausted, he stumbled to his horse and pulled out one of India's poultices. He examined his wound and was relieved that although large, it was not as deep as he previously thought. Gritting his teeth against the pain, he tightly wrapped the herb-filled gauze around the gash.

Looking around to ensure no other travelers were near, he realized del Cros had chosen this site well. It was well hidden, the perfect place for murder.

His heart still beat wildly, and his hands shook in nervous reaction to his deed. What now?

Taking another sip of water from his flask, he looked around and then back at the body. Should anyone come across it, they would surely assume that the man had fallen victim to thieves, but he couldn't in good conscience leave him like that. Taking the purse from Prades' horse, he loosened the reins and smacked his backend. The horse, skittish from the smell of blood, ran off into the brush, stopping a short distance away to nibble on some grass. Some lucky peasant would come across him soon enough.

Walking about, he found a number of good-sized boulders and set about the task at hand. Slowly and painfully aware that he was causing his gash to bleed more, he dragged the body over several feet towards a more secluded rocky area. A small gully of tall grasses provided the necessary screen, and he began to pile rocks on top of the body.

The laborious chore was completed only by taking several breaks and wincing through the pain. He wiped his brow and assessed his situation. He was not in good shape, and he still had one more task to do.

After building a small fire, he sat in front of it for a few minutes. He was anxious to leave the area, but the warmth and mesmerizing flickers of red and yellow flames provided momentary relief from the nightmare that had become his life. Feeling better, he reached into his satchel and took out the first sheet of vellum. Rereading every line and committing each word to memory, he fed it slowly into the fire, ensuring that it was reduced to ashes.

There, it was done.

Scuffing dirt into the fire with his boot until the flames were transformed into smoldering ashes and smoke, he looked around to be sure he had everything. Satisfied, he gingerly mounted his horse and pointed himself in the direction of Carcassonne. It was already late morning, and the fog had begun to burn off in the strong warm rays of the sun. It would be late by the time he arrived. He only hoped it would not be too dark. Exhausted and fearful about what he was returning to, he knew only that he was following his fate, wherever it led him.

Chapter Twenty-One

Favia was up early and preparing for the day. She had received word that Renier was coming today, and she nervously sliced her finger chopping onions. She did not like that man, or the way he looked at her. Today was pivotal to her future, and she was anxious about his arrival and their subsequent ruse.

She wondered how Prades was faring and whether he had managed to check out Jourdain's bags. She expected him to have returned already before Renier had noticed his absence. Either way she couldn't lose. No matter who found the money or treasure, she was bound to be paid. Tomorrow she could be a woman of leisure, and she rewarded herself with thoughts of all she would buy, including Prades' love.

* * * *

Renier dressed himself in plain, black clerical attire and looked at his image in the mirror. Despite a nose that was too long, he liked what he saw--a man of strength and cunning who was worthy of power, position and wealth. He smiled to himself. After today, he would have it all.

Del Cros had not returned last night from whatever tavern he was currently whoring at, and he was a miffed that the man was not here to breakfast with him. No matter, Prades was a bit of an idiot, despite his wit and charm.

His mind wandered toward what the day would unfold, and he thought of Favia. There was something about her that reminded him of someone, a face from his past, but he couldn't place who it was. Sauntering over to a table of food, he sliced off a thick slab of ham and walked to the window, while biting off a piece. The courtyard below was still heavy with fog, and here and there, movements of people carrying out chores could be observed within the shadowy mists. He saw a maid chasing a goose with a stick, and a beefy lad leading a horse in another direction, only to be engulfed a moment later into the fog. A milkmaid came into view, struggling with her pails, and he smiled down on her ample bosom.

Suddenly, he realized who Favia reminded him of. His first love. He began shivering with the excitement of possible ways for her to die.

* * * *

The heavy knock at the front door made Favia's heart pound and her palms sweat. Her stomach was already upset, and she had needed at least two cups of peppermint tea just to calm her nerves. She mutely stared at the door. Renier had arrived.

Unlatching the heavy bolt, she gave a quick look behind him, hoping to see Prades, and was disappointed to find him not there.

In the light, Renier seemed to be an even more distasteful creature. His black attire, contrasting starkly with his pale complexion, made him look more gaunt and thin than before. Blotchy red patches covered his nose, emphasizing the already large appendage. She mentally compared him to Prades who had a strong jaw, shapely calves and charming wit. Her confidence grew because she had been able to hold such an attractive man's attention. No matter who Renier was, whatever his title and occupation, he looked to be no more than a skinny, self-possessed ass with an enormous nose.

"Favia."

"Monsieur."

"I am here to see your mistress."

"She's upstairs, but who should I say is here to see her?"

"Tell her that an unknown gentleman is here, nothing more. I'll handle the rest."

In the moment it took for her to swing around, he grabbed her arm and held it tightly, his fingers pressing deeply into her skin.

"Not so fast. Del Cros didn't return home last night. You wouldn't know anything about that, would you?"

137

"Why would I know where Prades is?"

"I warned you. I'm not a man to be trifled with. If you know anything, I suggest you tell me now."

"Stop. You're hurting me. I don't know anything. He's probably off drunk somewhere."

"You'd better be right. I'd hate to think the two of you plotting away. Now go tell her I'm here."

Yanking her arm away from him, she scowled and then stomped her way up the stairs to India's room. Knocking lightly on the door, she entered to find the woman sitting in her usual spot by the window.

"Yes, Favia?" Uncharacteristically, India smiled, as she turned her head.

Something was off. The old woman seemed different as if she were daydreaming.

"There's a gentleman at the door to see you, Madame."

"A gentleman to see me? For what reason?"

"I've no idea, Madame. He simply says he wants to talk to you."

"He'll have to come up here, then. I've no intention of making my aching bones brave the stairs today."

"I'll show him up, then."

"Do we have any ale or wine to offer him?"

"No, Madame, but I'll run out to fetch some if you like."

"Do that, but be quick."

Stomping her wooden clogs down the stairs, Favia found Renier where she had left him "Follow me," she said.

He trailed her back up the stairs, his body odor overwhelming her as his body pressed against her back. There was no question that his purpose was to intimidate. As they arrived on the landing, she pointed to the door, expecting him to continue on his own. Instead, he held her back for a moment.

"Oh, and Favia?"

"Yes?"

"Take your time getting that wine."

* * * *

138

India could hear them coming up the stairs and overheard the brief request for Favia to take her time. Her visitor's tone certainly suggested more than a brief first meeting.

After a soft knock, he entered her room, and she eyed her unknown visitor with a mixture of curiosity and concern.

"Good day, Madame. My name is Jacques de Foix, a cleric in the legal trade. You will not know me, but you may have heard of my father, Guillaume de Foix?" He then turned around to ensure they were alone and whispered dramatically. "He was a strong Believer and bon chretien."

Watching him intently as he walked towards her, she fanned herself to relieve the rising heat in her face and neck. She guessed him to be in his late forties, obviously well-bred by his clothes, but by the looks of his clean, immaculate hands, he was not the cleric he said he was.

"Sit yourself, sir. My servant is out getting some wine. We are alone."

Her visitor's narrow lips curled into an almost imperceptible smile as he walked slowly to the window, coming uncomfortably closer.

"You have a most excellent view of the marketplace, Madame. Will she be long?"

"The streets are still crowded these days with pilgrims, so she may have to fight the crowds, but she'll be back soon enough. Plenty of time for you to state your business."

He briefly looked back at her, then turned and continued to gaze out the window.

"There's a chair over there for you."

"Ah, yes, merci." He slowly walked over to a carved rectangular chair. Sitting down, he delicately retrieved a lavender sachet from his cloak, inhaled a deep breath, smiled and nodded. "At last we meet, India Serras. I would imagine that you were beginning to wonder if I was ever going to arrive. I must admit it has taken some time to find you, but rest assured Madame, your long role as guardian is at a welcome end."

India narrowed her eyes and looked closely at her visitor. "To what are you referring, sir?"

His black, beady eyes targeted her own. "Come now, India, there's no need for secrets at such a late hour. I refer to the treasure spirited away from Montségur. I am here to relieve you of your heavy burden." Leaning forward, he smiled his voice soft, seductive and smooth. "I know it wasn't easy for you. It wasn't easy for any of us. I, too, lost family at Montségur. It was a painful time, and now there are so few of us left."

"Don't speak to me of Montségur, and who are you to take up my commission?"

"Granted, my appearance must come as a surprise. In truth, I swore an oath to my father on his deathbed to fulfill a promise he made to Bishop Marty. I only pray that I am not too late to honor that promise."

"And you've come here to collect it, is that it?"

"I've come to carry on the weight of your heavy burden."

India eyed him cautiously. The sound of feet clumping their way up the stairs was soon followed by a sound knock on the door. At last, Favia had returned.

"I have the wine for you," the woman called out.

Her visitor's mouth snapped into a thin smile as the servant entered. "Well done, miss. You're obviously well-skilled at fighting crowds."

"Just doing my job, sir." Carrying a tray with a large pewter vessel and two cups, Favia deposited everything on a bureau near de Beynac.

The two of them watched her as she brought each of them a cup of the warm, ruby liquid. Wiping her hands on her smock, the servant eyed this obvious imposter one last time and clomped her way back down the stairs. Not until she had heard every last step completed from Favia's wooden clogs, did India speak.

"What do you know of Montségur?"

There was an odd flicker in his eyes. "Only what was told to us by family members. I know the conditions were deplorable. I know two hundred and twenty Believers walked bravely to their burning pyre."

India studied him. The way he looked at her seemed familiar, somehow, and she stared harder.

"Were you there?"

"No, my family thought it best to send me to relatives in Aragon."

He was visibly agitated as he sat in his chair, and although he looked straight at her he was obviously uncomfortable talking about Montségur.

She might be nothing but a fool of an old woman, but she had spent a lifetime playing with the subtleties of truth.

"How fortunate for you. Were these relatives Believers or of the Roman faith?"

"My family is from a long line of Believers, Madame."

"Really, then, perhaps you can recite the Pater Nostre for my old ears. It has been years since I have heard it."

Instead of answering her right away, he fidgeted with his thumb and index finger, intently scratching at a hangnail in order to rip it off.

"Of course."

India smiled to herself. He looked for all the world like a ten-year-boy boy caught in a lie. His face was so familiar and she strained to remember from where. Then it struck her. She knew exactly where she had seen those eyes and why that boy knew her name. She had told him.

"You are quite right about Montségur. It was deplorable." India looked at him wide-eyed and fragile, as if he were her knight in shining armor. If this Jacques de Foix, cleric in the legal trade wanted to play games, she was more than ready to do so.

He changed the subject. "The escape must have been difficult."

"Yes, and I was terrified. I was also the only woman."

He had relaxed now that she was continuing her story. He leaned forward, captivated by her words, and arrogant enough to think she believed him.

"How many others escaped with you?"

"Initially there were four of us, but sadly not all made it."

"How many survived?"

"Only me."

"How dreadful. Please, go on. Tell me what happened."

"The first night I dared not stop, and so I continued on until dawn. The terrain was achingly difficult, and I found what looked like a safe refuge in the hollow of an overhanging outcrop of boulders. Wedging myself in as far as I could, I heaved an exhausted sigh and ate a wedge of stale bread. I remember taking only a nibble before falling into a deep, exhausted sleep.

"I was awakened the next morning by the sound of twigs breaking. When I saw a young boy wandering around, poking at bugs under a rock,

141

I was grateful for being well hidden or he could have come upon me as I slept. Then another young man came into the clearing. I cannot speak about what I unfortunately witnessed that day, but I have never forgotten that child's eyes or the unspeakable horror that he experienced."

She stared at him hard for full effect. "You know what they say, 'the dogs bark, but the caravan carries on'. "

The man began to cough and splutter from the wine. When he had regained his composure, it was not a fellow Believer that India saw staring back at her.

It was pure hate.

"I'm sure, Madame, there were many people at Montségur who found it deplorable. However, I am not here to talk about unspeakable deeds. The time has come to pass on the guardianship of the treasure."

"Indeed, it has, and I am glad for it. Your father must have died a happy man knowing that his son would carry on such a sacred mission. I presume then he also instructed you with everything?"

Her guest took another large gulp of wine as he steadily looked at her.

"Of course."

He spoke so softly she could barely hear him.

"Are you not afraid?" She asked.

"Afraid? Non. I trust in my faith and honoring my father's wishes."

"Then it is done. I happily acknowledge my role to be completed and yours to begin."

She then folded her hands in her lap and simply smiled at him. Not a word was spoken for several minutes, and his brows knit in obvious confusion.

"Are you not going to tell me where it is?"

"What do you mean 'where it is'? Didn't your father tell you?"

"Tell me what?"

"Where he hid it, of course."

"What are you saying?"

India had not felt this good in years and could barely restrain her eyes from twinkling. She had him now.

"Monsieur, did your illustrious father not tell you that it was he who hid the treasure, not me? Pity if he did not, for I have no idea where he would put such a thing."

Sputtering something she could not understand, he jumped to his feet, throwing the cup to the floor. "You're lying!"

"Monsieur, lying, as you well know, is against our religion. Perhaps when you make those accusations you should look a little closer to home."

His response was silence, but the raging storm inside him was breaking through into his quivering lower lip and the intensity of his black stare.

"I'm sorry I cannot help you, sir. I think it best that you leave and continue your search elsewhere. Perhaps your father left some written clue in his papers?"

"Enough. I'll leave for now, old woman, but I'll be back. I want that treasure, and you have no idea what I'm capable of doing to get it."

Instead of responding, she turned her head towards the window with thoughts of her son safe and far away. She smiled.

* * * *

Renier stormed down the stairs, rage evident in every pore of his reddened face. Watching from below, Favia had the tiniest of smirks on her face. So, he had been bested by the old lady? Unfortunately, for her, Renier caught the look, and before she could turn and get out of the way, his hand was around her wrist in a flash.

Twisting her arm around her back, he yanked it upwards, his other arm tightened around her neck. "Here's a little warning for you, poppet. If I find out that you and India have made a deal, I'll slit you from ear to ear. You hear me? I'll be back tomorrow, and I expect to know where the treasure is. Got it?"

"How am I supposed to find that out?"

His breath was rancid, and she almost gagged as he leaned closer to whisper in her ear.

"Now, now, Favia. We both know that you're a very clever girl. I'm sure you'll think of something. Oh, and Favia?"

With tears in her eyes, she squeaked out a timid, "Yes?"

"I'd better see Prades by that time, too."

* * * *

Weary, Jourdain drew his cloak closer and leaned forward on his horse. He had continued riding towards Carcassonne despite the pain in his side. He had to ensure India was okay.

Leading his horse through the city gates just before they closed for the night, he thought back to the last time he had done this only weeks ago. How his life had changed in that time. How he had changed.

He had no formal plan. He would bribe Favia with coins, and then sort out what he needed to do after that. For the second time in his life, tired and in great pain, he arrived at India's doorstep and gave a deep, loud knock.

Chapter Twenty-Two

Favia was stirring the last of the embers in the scullery when a knock sounded on the door. Thinking it was Prades returning with their reward, she raced to the door before India awoke and got nosey. Flushed with the anticipation, she opened the door with a wide smile that froze at first glance.

"Jourdain."

"Favia."

Looking behind him for some explanation, she stumbled over her words. "You're back."

Gingerly stepping through the door, he winced and spoke sharply. "Clever of you to notice. Get Pierre to see to my horse. Then we need to talk. Just you and me."

Favia caught sight of his dark blood-soaked shirt and gasped. "What happened?"

"I am weary, irritable and in no mood for your feigned innocence at this late hour. You know very well what happened. You sent del Cros after me."

"I don't know what you're talking about."

"You're lying because he admitted it, and you might as well know right now that he's dead."

She could feel the blood draining from her cheeks. Her heart grew faint with fear, and her knees weakened. "That's not true, you're lying."

Jourdain looked down at his bloodied clothes and back to her. "This gash is not a lie."

"What do you want? You can't prove I had anything to do with him."

"To start with, I have no intention of having this conversation in the doorway. I am tired and in pain. I want to know that India is safe. I want my horse taken care of. I want some warm broth and cold ale. Then, and only then, will you and I have a conversation in the scullery to discuss a deal. You will do this all now and with quick action. Do I make myself clear?"

Favia's eyes widened. This was not the man who had left with his tail between his legs only the day before. He had a new voice, and even though he was tired, it sounded deeper, richer and more confident. Somehow, he even looked taller. She took a step back. It would seem that she had underestimated him, but she wouldn't let it happen again. She'd listen to his deal, then make her own if it didn't suit her.

* * * *

It took some time before everything was completed. Jourdain reassured himself that India was indeed safe by slowly climbing the stairs as quietly as he could manage and looking in on her. Holding his breath, he tilted his head forward in an effort to hear her softly exhaling. It reminded him of when he would stare at Leo's cradle, barely able to resist the urge to wake him to ensure he was still breathing. For now, she was safe. He then made his way to the scullery.

He silently ate the broth that awaited him at the end of the table, while Favia crossed her arms and watched. His gash needed attending to, but he would not give her the satisfaction of seeing del Cros's handiwork.

"Thank you. Now, you and I will have our chat."

Favia looked at him with stone-faced anger in her eyes. He had no doubts that she hated him. So be it.

"We have an accord. You want money. I want India's safety, and I am willing to pay you well for your silence."

"You don't fool me. Why should you care about India? You only want the money like the rest of us."

"What do you mean by the rest of us? Who else knows about this?"

"No one. I swear. It was only Prades and I, until you murdered him."

"I shouldn't need to remind you, Favia, that it was me defending myself against a murderer. As for caring for India, it is only right that a

146

son cares for his aging mother.'"

"What?"

"You heard me. I am her only son and legal heir. You can hope for nothing more than what I offer you now."

Favia let the words sink in before she pouted out an answer. "Get on with it, then. What is India's dutiful son willing to pay for a scullery maid's silence?"

Reaching into the satchel, he drew out a heavy bag of coins and dropped them on the table before her. "More than what you deserve."

Favia looked at the del Cros monogram on the bag, and then back to Jourdain's eyes. There was no bargaining in them, no way to get whatever else was in the satchel. Looking back at the leather sack of coins, she judged them to be enough to provide her with an exit from India's household. Besides, she knew exactly where to get more. It would be a bargain with the devil, but this was information Renier would pay for.

"I accept your deal then." Putting her hand on the sack, she attempted to take it.

His hand dropped suddenly on hers. "Swear you will leave tomorrow and say nothing to anyone?"

Favia looked at him and smiled. "I swear." Leaning forward, she loosened her hand from his clutch and then slid the sack onto her lap, where it landed with a thud and the pleasant sound of her future.

"I will hold you to that. I am to bed, and I'll warn you now, the door will be locked. Try anything, and you'll join your Prades before the night is through. Understand?"

"I have what I want, Jourdain, as do you. I'll be gone by morning. Sleep well."

Waiting until she was sure he was asleep, Favia donned her dusty ragged cloak and headed into the night. What she had to say could not wait until morning when Renier was sure to return. What she had to offer was worth double what Jourdain had given her, and she was determined to ensure her future was as brightly as she imagined.

* * * *

Prades had not yet returned to his home, and Renier was getting more frustrated by the minute. It had not gone well today, and he suspected he had been double-crossed. There was no question that India had recognized him and played along with his lie. A memory like that was the devil's work. Her age alone was witchcraft at the very least.

He paced in an effort to relax and forget his failed meeting with India. He didn't feel like himself right now. He felt exposed, like that moment when he first saw her eyes at Montségur. Pouring himself another drink, he awaited word from the third servant of Prades about the whereabouts of his master. Nothing was going as planned.

It was late in the evening when a servant announced a visitor at the door.

"Who is it?"

The man curled his lip in disgust. "The same young female as before, sir."

Renier smiled. "Favia. Send her in. I'd be quite interested in speaking with that little bitch right now."

Ushering her into the salon, the servant checked to see if he needed anything more, nodded his head, shut the doors and left.

"I see you haven't wasted any time." He stopped his pacing and looked at Favia. He probably smelled of wine, and his words were slurring a little, but he didn't care. "What news do you bring now?"

"I thought I would find you here. But don't bother to wait because Prades is dead."

"What did you say?"

"I said, Prades is dead."

"How do you know this?"

"Jourdain returned tonight and told me so. He said Prades followed him, and I presume he tried to rob him. He was killed in the fight."

Renier narrowed his eyes and moved closer to Favia.

"Why would Prades follow Jourdain, and what was he robbing him of?"

"I don't know, sir."

Renier's lower lip quivered with an attempt to restrain his anger. "What do you mean you don't know?" Each word was staccato sharp, edged with rage.

Taking a step back, Favia cowered against the chair. "I don't know.

I really don't."

In an instant, he had covered the space between them and slapped her hard against her face. "You're lying."

Crying and holding her inflamed cheek, she whimpered in defense. "If I had anything to do with it, why would I come and tell you? He obviously tried to cheat you, and I thought you should know. Besides that, I have even more important information that you will want to hear."

"Out with it before I lose my patience."

"Jourdain said that he is India's son and legal heir."

"Why didn't you tell me this before?"

"I didn't know. He's only just told me, and I've come here. I think India's the one who's put that in his head, so who knows if it's true?"

Renier furled his brow and stopped. He needed to take in this new information, so he found a seat by the fire. Picking up his cup of wine, he savored a long slow sip while watching Favia.

"So what you are saying to me is that Jourdain is India's son, and whether it's true or not, both she and he seem to believe it. Prades followed Jourdain to steal something, but we don't know what that is, and you, of course, had nothing to do with it. Prades was killed in the process, and Jourdain has returned to India with possibly whatever it was that Prades was trying to steal. Am I correct so far?"

Wiping her nose across her sleeve, Favia merely nodded.

"You are here, I further presume, to collect on that information, and leave, never to be seen or heard from again."

"I am, sir, yes."

Renier leaned forward, poured himself more wine, and slowly rose to his feet, cup in hand. This was going to be all too easy, and he shivered in anticipation. He mustn't rush through it this time, though, and not make such a mess. Hands shaking, he sat beside her. She was as nervous as a hare caught in a trap, but she wanted her money so she'd let him get close. For the right amount, she'd probably let him do whatever he wanted, especially now that del Cros was dead. He knew this already, for this was a game that he played well.

Lifting his quivering hand, he stroked her face and cooed, "You were a very good girl to tell me all this."

She fidgeted, pursed her lips and couldn't look him in the eye. She played with a lock of hair before she answered. "Yes, sir."

He continued to stroke her face, then slowly began to trace his finger down towards her bodice to the bare flesh that rose above her kirtle, waiting to see if she would resist. She squirmed a little but did nothing to move his hand. All the better.

"Tell me, Favia. Who else knows you are here?"

Her breathing became faster. "No one, sir."

He closed his eyes and visibly shivered. His hand shook as he widened his fingers and spread his hand fully over her young breast. "Won't they miss you?"

Her face was flushed, and her hands fussed with her skirts. He had his prey right where he wanted her.

"No. I've been let go."

He leaned in closer to her neck, the better to smell the intoxicating aroma of panicking fear.

"I see." No one would be looking for her.

"Please, sir, I promise you, you'll never see me again, and I'll speak to no one."

His voice was silk and smooth. "Oh, I already know that, Favia. Have you by chance seen Prades' private rooms upstairs?"

"No, sir."

"Perhaps you'd like to see them with me? I'm sure you'll feel more comfortable there, non?"

"Will you pay me afterwards?"

"Everything you deserve and more."

Renier entered the rooms first, noting that the servants had laid a fire and left wine, no doubt used to Prades' late hours. The nobleman's apartments were richly enough attired, but the fabrics were badly in need of replacement. Carved chests and bureaus surrounded the room along with several woven wall hangings that were threadbare with moths and age. No wonder he needed money.

Flames from the candles danced shadows against the heavy drapes that hung from a large pillared bed. Renier watched Favia take it all in and was aware he would be a lesser specimen in her eyes to Prades, but no matter. His sword could penetrate just as well, and that would be the last thing this slut would remember.

He circled around behind her, clasped her arms and whispered in her ear. "You're not in a hurry, I hope. I would expect you'll be here for most of the night before you, how shall I put it, leave us for good?"

"Why did you say it like that?"

"Say what?"

"Leave us for good. You want a tumble? Okay, but you're going to pay me and let me leave, right?"

"No, Favia, that is not right. You see, I can't let that happen. Now, now, I can see the fear in your eyes, but I assure you I've been very thoughtful. After all, where else but Prades' bed would you rather die?"

"I'll scream."

"Scream away. All the better. Do you really think you're the only tart that rogue has had in his chamber? Imagine how surprised they'll be to find a dead woman in his bed by his hand, and he gone missing. Tidies things up nicely, don't you think?"

"You're mad. Nobody will believe it. Prades was a gentleman and more of a man than you'll ever be."

Renier shook from head to toe. His pulse raced, and his heart pounded. "What did you just say?"

"He's more of a man dead than you are alive. Look at you, nothing but a milksop. You're obviously incapable of even being with a woman, or perhaps you prefer little boys?"

He pounced. Blood rushed through his head, putting pressure behind his eyes, blinding out her screams. His hand around her neck, he tested each fragile slender bone and his pulse raced with the power. Pressing a little harder, he almost felt giddy as her eyes began to bulge. He had to control his breathing so as to not rush this pleasure. Little squeaking noises escaped from her mouth. Her arms flailed in an attempt to escape his clutch, and he could no longer control himself.

She clawed at his face, tried to rip his hands from her throat. She was a hellcat, a fighting fish, a trapped rabbit in his hands. She was a milkmaid in his father's barn, and in one rush of explosive ecstasy of that memory he pressed as hard as he could until she struggled no more. His entire body shuttered in release.

Satiated and spent, he needed a moment to regain his clarity. Smiling, he staggered over to a nearby chair. Their greed had definitely worked in his favor, and he was pleased. He had only to casually mention that del Cros had arrived home late, then discover Favia along with everyone else.

Throwing her lifeless body on the nobleman's bed, he took a deep gulp of wine, looked back once, and then slipped off to his own rooms to sleep. Tomorrow would be a very busy day.

Chapter Twenty-Three

India awoke the following morning to something she never expected to see—Jourdain asleep on a chair, his satchels beside him.

"Jourdain?"

"You're awake."

"What are you doing here?"

"I'm taking you home with me if you're able. If not, I'll stay here as long as I need to."

She shook her head, as she furled her brow. "No. You need to leave. I need to keep you safe. Don't you understand? You're in danger if you stay."

"I know that, but my conscience will be in far more danger if I don't."

"Does Favia know you're back?"

"There's very little that Favia doesn't know, I assure you, but I've given her enough coin to buy her silence. I heard her sneak out late last night, so I doubt we'll be seeing her again."

India nodded. "Good. I'll need some help getting out of this bed. Can you take my hand?"

Jourdain rose slowly and took her hand, but the moment he exerted any effort to pull her up, he visibly winced from the pain in his side. India immediately let go of his clutch.

"You're hurt."

"I am, but not seriously. I've put one of your poultices on it for now. You can look at it later."

"Men." India shook her head. I'll be looking at it now, if you don't mind." With some maneuvering, she managed to get herself into a

153

standing position, grabbed her cane and gave him a stern, motherly look. "Well? Lift your shirt and show me." Pressing the dried poultice with her finger, she nodded her assessment. "Just as I thought, I'm going to have to soften that up before I take it off. The blood has caked it to your skin. It'll be impossible to take off as it is." Giving him a wry smile, she shook her head again. "You are your father's son, that's for sure. How did this happen?"

"Favia and a friend of hers named Prades del Cros. He followed me with the intent of stealing the satchel. We fought. He would have killed me had I not killed him first."

"I have no doubt of that. Did anyone see you?"

"No, it was a secluded location of his choosing."

India looked in his eyes and surmised what he was not saying. "You were careless, and it almost cost you your life."

He nodded. "It's true, but it won't happen again. In the space of a month, I have been accosted twice, and twice I've felt the slice of a cold blade into my skin. I narrowly escaped death both times. I will not taunt the powers that be with a third."

"That, my son, would be wise. I may not be around for the third. Now help me to the scullery. We need plenty of water to soften up that poultice. Afterwards, we need to talk. There are still things I need to tell you about what you carry."

It took the better part of the morning to see to Jourdain's slash, but only when she was satisfied that he had not severed anything major did she tightly bind him up. His other injury was mending well, and she patted his arm in satisfaction.

"Shall we grab that last heel of bread and some wine and sit in the solar? I had a visitor of my own that I suspect involves Favia."

A sudden banging on the door stopped them both in their tracks, and they anxiously flashed a look at one another. Neither moved to see if the visitor would knock again. This time it was louder, stronger, more insistent. Jourdain turned to India.

"That's not Favia," he said.

"No, I'll expect it to be someone else. Let him in. Jourdain. I don't suppose I could convince you to take that satchel and flee?"

"No. Whoever this is, we'll deal with them together."

"I thought as much. Then I'll make my way to the solar. Invite our guest there, but first make sure your dagger is close by."

"It has never left my boot."

She looked up at her son's face in search of his father's strength and found it in his eyes. "Answer the door then."

She knew exactly who it was. Death had come to collect her at last.

* * * *

Renier was in no mood to wait. Banging on the door a third time, he was rewarded with the sound of the bolt being roughly pulled aside before he was through.

The man who opened the door was slight, but not without muscle. His face was strong, his eyes direct.

"What do you want?"

So this was India's son. "I am Renier de Beynac, the lead inquisitor to his Excellency Pope Clement, and I am here to speak to India Serras. And you are?"

"Jourdain, Madame Serras's son."

"Really. Then I'll need to speak with you as well."

"She's in the solar."

"How pleasant. I'll follow you in."

Renier walked into the room, taking note of India already seated in a chair by the fire. Today there would be no pretending, no bargaining. By the time he left this house, they'd both be dead, and he would be a very powerful man.

"India, a pleasure to see you again." He broadened his smile and offered her a perfunctory bow of courtesy. "I've already met your son. A very nice surprise, I must say, and his father?"

India's eyes followed him around the room.

"He died at Montségur."

"Pity."

Jourdain stood sentinel behind his mother, hands resting on the back of her chair as Renier continued looking around the room. Spying the other chair, he sat down and smiled at the two of them. "I'll sit here if it's all right with you?"

"What is it you want?"

"I think that's a very easy question to answer. Why don't we ask your mother? Why am I here, India?"

"You want the treasure, but I told you yesterday your father hid it."

"We both know that's a lie, India." He tightened his mouth, dismissing the pasted on smile, and narrowed his eyes. "I know it's not the truth because I'm not a cleric. I'm also no longer the unfortunate little boy you met at Montségur. With the Pope's blessing, I burn people like you and am very well rewarded for it. Actually, you may find this somewhat amusing, Jourdain, but I suspect it would have been my father who lit the pyre that sent your father to hell."

In two strides, Jourdain had grabbed a handful of cloth by Renier's neck and jerked him to a standing position.

"Jourdain, watch out," India screamed. It was too late.

Anticipating his outburst, Renier pulled out a dagger from under his cloak and held the point to Jourdain's neck. A small push caused a trickle of blood to trail down as Jourdain's hands swung high, his palms out in surrender. Their eyes locked in hate.

"Don't move."

India paled.

Renier smirked and held Jourdain there, relishing the power. He would have loved to run him through right then and there, but he needed the man alive, for now.

"Where's the treasure, India? I warn you, think twice before you tell me another lie because I'll slash his throat before your very eyes."

"Some of it is here. The rest is hidden," she replied in a voice heavy with defeat.

"Hidden where?" he demanded, smiling to himself.

"Let him go, and I'll tell you."

"Tell me now, or he dies."

"Kill him, and I will tell you nothing." The strength of conviction returned to her voice.

Renier reconsidered her words. Pressing his knife a little deeper, he smiled as Jourdain winced and a fresh rivulet of blood trailed down his neck.

"I'll bet you know where it is, don't you?" He watched his prey closely.

Jourdain's eyes shifted. "I do not."

It was all the confirmation he needed. He doubted her son would hold out very long at the sight of his mother being gutted.

"You said some of it is here. Where?" He looked at India.

"In the satchel," she replied, her voice wobbling.

In an instant, he lifted his foot to Jourdain's groin and with a well-placed heave pushed him to the floor. He leapt over to India, his knife inches away from her exposed neck. "Tell him to get it."

India's eyes looked to Jourdain for a full minute before nodding her assent.

Jourdain looked from Renier to India and spat his frustration. In a moment, he was back with the sack hanging from his fingers. Placing it in India's lap, he backed away.

Renier eyed the weather-worn leather and recognized it as the same one he had seen years ago in India's possession. He wanted to grab it and marvel at what priceless treasures he had acquired but he restrained himself.

"Open it."

India did as she was told and slowly opened the bag wide enough to reveal four silk-wrapped items.

Renier couldn't stand it and grabbed what looked to be a book. He threw off the silk covering and read the cover from the ancient tome. "*Ignis.*" Turning to the first page, he quickly skimmed over its contents while keeping one eye on Jourdain.

"One of the four essential books of alchemy."

He smiled and turned to India. "I take it that the *Table of Testimony* and the gospel era *Jerusalem Manuscripts* are well hidden? How I will look forward to reading them, my dear. My understanding is that the manuscripts hold enough substance of information to expose the fundamental concept of the Catholic Church. How useful that information will be. This myth of Jesus has served us well, non?"

She simply nodded.

"You realize, India, that this book alone would be grounds for me to declare you a heretic and have you burned at the stake? Give me the other one."

Grabbing it out of her hand, he threw off the silk cover to reveal what he had hoped to find *Feuilles de Bois*—the wooden pages. Carefully, he opened the cover to reveal a thick set of parchment pages. Depictions of animals and geometric shapes were interspersed with an ancient script. "The vanished *Naadis* said to reveal the true lineage of Jesus and his descendants." To think his father had ordered the fortress of Montségur dismantled brick by brick just to find this very book. He was barely able to restrain himself now. This alone was worth killing them both.

"Give me that small box," he barked at India, his hand shaking.

India caught Jourdain's eye long enough for him to notice.

"What's in there?"

Her eyes lowered, and she mumbled her reply.

"Speak up, or I'll slit your throat here and now."

Jourdain looked as if he were about to pounce. No matter. He had only half of what he wanted, and India was still the key to getting the rest. He wasn't about to murder India for the mere pleasure of seeing Jourdain's face crumble, at least not yet.

"A cup." She bit her lip and looked to Jourdain. "The Grail."

Renier could hardly believe his ears.

"Open it."

Taking a deep breath, India pulled out the silk wrapped box from the satchel and offered it to Renier.

"I said, open the box then hand it to me."

"As you wish." Her voice was quiet, and she once again caught Jourdain's eye.

Unwrapping the silk, revealed an ornately carved wooden casket about double the size of a large man's fist. In the front lay a tiny clasp, which she easily moved aside. She swung the lid open and it fell back on its hinges revealing a smaller object wrapped in deep, purple velvet.

Renier could barely breathe.

Carefully unwrapping the velvet, India hesitated, then held out the cup to him. Jourdain leaned forward to look before Renier growled a warning. Renier stared at the cup in her hands and was disappointed. This was no silver or jeweled encrusted vessel. Instead lay a common enough turned alabaster cup.

"Give it to me."

His prize in hand, he turned it over to see if it was carved or inscribed in some way. It was not. He turned to India.

"You lie," he said, venom in his voice. "This is no treasure. It's nothing but an old cup." He made to throw it into the fire, but the look of horror on her face made him stop.

"It is the Grail, I swear. It looks different to everyone. You just haven't claimed ownership. You are not yet its master."

He looked from Jourdain to India, both their faces serious, frightened. He nodded his head in the old woman's direction.

"Tell me."

"You need to drink wine from it, the way that Jesus did. In that way He was able to resurrect and overcome the limitations of His physical body."

"What will it do to me?"

"Besides immortal life, whatever you ask of it, but first you must claim it for your own."

"Tell your son to fetch me wine."

India looked to Jourdain and took a deep breath. "Look in the scullery. Favia bought some yesterday and there may well still be a jug."

Jourdain returned with a half-full vessel and scowled at Renier as he handed it to India.

Renier curled a smile and looked down his nose to India. "Fill it, then, slowly hand it to me."

India began to cough, and he had to wait until her breathing subsided before she continued.

A vein in his temple throbbed in frustration. "Get on with it!"

Her hands shaking, she filled the cup, spilling some of the wine on the outside as a result. Grabbing it from her hands before she spilled anything more, he frowned to see his fingers splotched with wine stains. No matter. There was nothing he could do about it now.

He slowly put the cup to his lips and watched India from the corner of his eye. He stopped. Was that a hint of a smile?

"Do you really think me so foolish as to drink poison? Tell your son to drink some of that wine first."

Jourdain looked over to his mother, and without any hesitation grabbed the flask and took a swig. His eyes burned into Renier's as he wiped his mouth with his sleeve.

"There."

"And you, India, you're next."

Renier waited for a few minutes, taking the opportunity to slowly wipe the spots off his hands, until he was satisfied that the wine was safe. "Thank you both for your cooperation. I have learned you see that one can never be too careful."

Holding the cup with both hands, he raised it above his head. Thinking only of ultimate power and wealth, he drank to his future.

It took only a moment to realize something was very wrong. He began to cough, sputter, and then sweat profusely. His face contorted in pain, he screamed, "It burns! It burns! You bastard, I'm burning inside!" Clawing at his neck, he made a grab for the wine in India's hands but met only her steel blue eyes and a pool of red on the floor beside her.

In a last desperate bid to control his situation, he grasped his knife and blindly stabbed in India's direction, but it was already too late. In a fit of coughing, frothy bloody bubbles flowed from his mouth. He fell to the floor in front of her, his one hand pawing at his throat, the other clutching her skirt. His last breath inhaled the smell of soured rushes. His last memory was of India's smiling face.

Stunned, Jourdain's mouth dropped open.

"Are you all right?" he asked India.

"Yes."

"The cup was poisoned?"

"Yes." Suddenly his mother began to cough and gasp for air.

He looked at the goblet that had tumbled onto the floor and back at India. She, too, had held the Grail.

Frantically dragging Renier's body away from his mother, he knelt and grasped her hand. The coughing had subsided, and as she looked at him, she patted his arm and smiled.

"There's not much time, and I have things I need to say."

He felt useless, frustrated and impatient to do something, anything.

"Just tell me what I can do," he said, his voice breaking.

"Nothing but listen."

"But you're a Guardian. Why would the Grail kill you?"

"Because, dear one, it is not the Grail. It is only a copy."

"Why did you touch it, then?

"Renier was already suspicious, and it was the only way to blind him to anything but his greed for power."

"How did you know I wouldn't?"

"You wouldn't have opened it, much less drunk from it, because you are the next Keeper. I told you, the Grail protects its own. Besides, there was no time to explain everything. I wrote only what I safely could. Everything you need to know will be in that cave."

He ran his hands through his hair. "You trusted me."

"Of course, I trusted you. I still trust you. Now be quiet, and let me speak." She coughed a little more, her eyes reflecting pain. "You understand my letter and what lays hidden in that cave?"

"Yes, I think so."

"Good, because it is far more than what you could possibly imagine. You think you'll be able to find it?"

"It won't be easy, but I should be alright as long as I repeat your steps and then use that Roman well as a guide."

"Look for the mark chiseled on a rock just outside to the right. You'll know that it's the correct one, once you're inside." She winced again and grabbed his hand squeezing it tightly. "Promise me. Promise your father that you will do this."

"I will, but what can I do to help you? Whatever you need, I'll get it."

"Just listen. Although the books and parchments are priceless, it is the knowledge they contain that is the true treasure." She looked at him and smiled, though by her eyes it was clear she was in great agony.

"You'll have a lifetime of learning ahead of you so take no more than two books at a time. The two that you have are the last two I was able to take out before my health began to fail me. The one, *Ignis,* has been my constant companion these good many years. The other, the wooden book, must not fall into the wrong hands. I would see that one safely with the others first." She pursed her lips, the pain obviously peaking, and she had to wait until it subsided before she began again. "There is one more thing that you must do. After I am gone, I want you to take my ashes and spread them on the 'camp de cremat' at Montségur.

This is something you must promise me you will do, for only there will my soul be completely free."

She looked into his eyes deeply, her forehead furled in pain.

His heart nearly broke. To lose her now after only just finding her was unthinkable.

"It is where your father promised that he will be waiting for me. You will do this for me, yes?"

"I promise." He looked down at her hand in his and bent his forehead nodding his assent.

Her moist eyes began to shine, her focus drifting as she pressed his hand and whispered, "It's beautiful in that cave, like a cathedral. I painted it just like the other one."

Then she closed her eyes and was gone.

It took a minute for Jourdain to register what had just happened. He held his breath and watched her face for any signs of life. There was none. He felt lost and alone, like an abandoned little boy.

Using India's chair as leverage, he grasped the frame and slowly raised himself until he stood, unsure what to do next. He looked at Renier lying dead on the floor, his face contorted into a final moment of pain, and then back at India, whose peaceful smile graced her face. An overwhelming flood of emotions--rage, frustration and anguish-- swept over him as he realized it was all over. Staggering a few steps, he dropped his head, pounded his hands raw against the wall and sobbed.

Chapter Twenty-Four

A month later, Jourdain found himself near the small mountain village of Montségur. He had India's ashes and one last unread memoire he had found in his satchel. He looked up towards the Pog and the arduous climb ahead. It was mid-afternoon on a hot August day and climbing a steep rocky mountainside was not going to be so easy. Checking that his flask held sufficient water, he bent his head and began the long ascent.

The path had obviously not been used for many a year since bushes and thickets blocked his way. The going was slow, but the landscape around him was breathtaking. It was a good excuse to stop now and then, to catch his breath and take a drink.

He had considered securing a guide from the village for help, but this was something he needed to do himself. It was best not to attract any further attention.

He continued to climb until dusk, worried that he wouldn't find the 'camp de cremat' before dark. Then he found himself on a flat, peaceful meadow. A simple wooden cross with the carved outline of a dove was his confirmation that he was where he needed to be. Relieved, he looked around. A sacred place, it surely must be, for the very air seemed to still and hush at his arrival.

The sun was low on the horizon as he viewed moss-carpeted boulders circling around the meadow like centurions guarding a sacred temple. Lush ferns hung from the banks nourished by the mountain mists. He closed his eyes and inhaled a deep breath of the sweet mountain air.

In a short time, the sun dropped behind the chain of rugged tors, reducing their jagged heights to deep purple shadows framed against the red of the late summer sky. Darkness was quickly approaching, and he took a walk around in order to find a spot to rest that would not be so exposed. It didn't take long. Finding a small copse with a boulder to rest his back against, he immediately found comfort by stretching out his legs and grabbing his flask of water.

Closing his eyes, he thought about the past month. He had managed to send word to Maura that he was safe and would soon be home. He felt a world away from his old life for so much about him had changed. Where was the man who worried about the cost of leather or whether they had enough to eat over the winter months? Where was the man who fretted about what he should and shouldn't believe? He smiled to himself and released a deep sigh. He felt free.

He had initially thought that Renier's body would present the bigger challenge, but the generous coin he offered to the cart-bearers ensured his "uncle's" eternal rest in a peasant's grave, unmarked and forgotten. His promise to India had been a far more difficult task, but he had complied with her wishes and now here he was at this place of such great sorrow.

Taking a drink, he shifted his weight to relieve the strain on his side, healed but still sore, and then took a deep breath. He had been worried about how he would react when he got here, but he was surprisingly relaxed. He had wondered whether he would feel his father's presence. He didn't. There was no sense of tortured souls or restless spirits. There were no echoes of battle drums or the ghostly monks singing the "Veni Creator Spiritus" as families walked willingly into a mass burning pyre. There was just the peacefulness of a sleepy meadow soon to be under a blanket of the night's stars.

Reaching into his satchel, he pulled out the unread letter and a small loaf of rough bread, ripped off a large wedge and finished it in only a few bites. He hadn't realized how hungry he was. He eyed the heel, but decided to eat it later. Tomorrow he would treat himself to a proper meal, like a big bowl of the local cassoulet. Unfolding India's last letter, he settled himself to read.

Mémoires de India Serras

164

The last ceremony was to begin after night had fallen, and we were to congregate as best we could in the open courtyard. Despite the shifting bodies, there was an eerie silence, for everyone knew they would nevermore see stars or feel the cool night air. Tomorrow, at dawn's light, their souls would be released. Everyone would die.

The Perfects moved from family to family, giving a nod, a blessing, a warm embrace to the woman softly weeping as she held her child, and another to the woman with the vacant stare, for her baby no longer cried. I watched in silence as the Perfects comforted her and felt her pain as she fell to her knees weeping. I remember the feeling of guilt, for their fate would not be mine.

Bishop Marty had begun to address everyone and stood in a central place where he could best be seen.

"Ecouté! Listen! On this last night, it is important for us all to examine our hearts and souls. As you know, everyone has three natures: the body, which is the abode of the soul; the soul, which is the abode of the spirit; and the spirit, which is the divine spark. The reason we dedicate our life to purity is so this spark, which has been nourished in our souls, will separate at our death and return to the light. This is what will happen to each of you tomorrow.

"As simple Believers you've lived fully in the ways of the world, but now, in order to prepare your souls for their final release and reunion with the Divine Spark, you are making the conscious choice to live in purity, love and faith, and it will thus be done."

A sea of affirmations swept across the courtyard like a wave.

Marty continued. "Hence it is meet and right that you be resolved in your heart to keep this Holy Prayer all your life, according to the custom of the Church of God, in purity and truth, and in all other virtues which God would bestow upon you.

Wherefore we pray the good Lord, who bestowed upon the disciples of Jesus Christ the virtue to receive this Holy Prayer steadfastly, that He may grant to you also the grace to receive it steadfastly, in His honour.

If ye forgive not men their trespasses, neither will your Heavenly Father, forgive your trespasses.

Good Christians we pray you by the love of God that you grant this blessing, which God had given you, to our friends here present. By God and by us and by the Church, may your sins be forgiven and we pray God to forgive you them"

Adoremus, Patrem, et Filium et Spiritum Sanctam.
Adoremus, Patrem, et Filium et Spiritum Sanctam.
Adoremus, Patrem, et Filium et Spiritum Sanctam.

I will never forget the overwhelming feeling of sacredness as in unison we chanted the responses to the prayers, and I know that Montségur will forever hold the memory of our gathering in its heart. I truly understood that night what it meant to be Cathar~to understand that I was a part of the divine spark. I was proud of their choice, and if we must part, this would be the best of good-byes. I looked around to see peaceful smiling faces. Surrounded by these gentle-hearted believers, tears filled my eyes. These were my people of my faith, and I would do whatever it took to honor and remember them.

I write so that those who have gone before me do not die without memory or purpose. I write to give them form, voice, song and laughter. I write to remind myself that they lived, and that once, long ago, gentle Cathars like me were free to love, live and believe as freely as the dove flies high over the fields and mountains of the Pyrenees.

Jourdain, my soul was dead these fifty long years. Numbed to fear, I merely existed day-to-day waiting for another to guard. It somehow excused me from keeping my promise. Time passed, until one day I realized that perhaps one day the "Guardian" would never come. I realized that I would one day pass on as well, and then no one would ever know the truth. Then you found me.

"Remember me," Amidée my brave little girl with big brown eyes had said, and I had promised I would remember everything. I would remember how women chatted and gossiped as they washed laundry at the forks, or did other chores. I also would remember the tiny blue flowers that grew beside Marie's stone hut, the heady bouquet of apple blossoms in the spring, the smell of damp earth, the memory of the blood red sky as their bodies burned, and finally, the silence afterwards.

Who would be alive to tell their tales, their lives? Only me. History will have forgotten us long after my life is gone, and my words are no longer even an echo on the hills, but the fact remains that we lived, we loved and we existed. The truth did not die along with our cloaks of flesh.

Deeply moved, Jourdain closed his eyes to think about her words, but the day's climb had tired him and he fell asleep. It was dark and late when he was jolted awake by a startled grouse that had wandered too close. Attracted by a stray bread crumb, the bird flapped his wings then swooped through the bushes, weaving in and out.

It took a minute to still his heartbeat, but once calmed, he rubbed his eyes, stretched his back and looked around. The moon was large and full, casting an eerie glow to the low mist that now clung to the meadow floor. Stars blanketed the sky, and there was complete silence. He sat there for a few minutes slowing his breath and straining his ears to hear anything at all, and in that moment he knew. It was time.

Taking the carefully wrapped vessel from his satchel, he stood and walked towards the center of the meadow. The grass was soft and cool to walk on, and the mist swirled playfully around his feet. The moonlit night marked a path for him and just when he reached his destination a small gust of wind caused wisps of his hair to caress his cheek.

Lifting the waxen lid from the vessel, he raised his arms. The ashes, held aloft, were stirred by the gentle breeze. He smiled and was whispering his goodbyes when suddenly he stopped and stared hard into the night.

In front of him, the mist had started to thicken into a forest of growing spirals, slowly swirling, raising themselves in height at every turn. He was spellbound and a little frightened, but he couldn't stop watching. The columns continued to swirl into various heights, and then just as suddenly stopped. In that same moment, depth and detail began to seep in. Hands, arms, shoulders and faces began to take form until he could clearly see a young couple and a host of men, women and children behind them, all silently staring at him. The couple slowly moved towards him, then stopped. Looking at the young woman's eyes, he smiled. He would recognize that twinkle anywhere.

"Mother."

"Jourdain." Her voice was as soft as a caress. She looked toward the young man beside her, and with misty eyes, she took his hand and brought it to her heart. "Jourdain, this is your father. Durand, this is our boy."

The man, his father, stood tall and smiled back at him. His face was a chiseled portrait of deep love, loyalty and strength that could easily command men with a single word. This was a man who anyone would be proud to have as a father. He felt like a little boy, inadequate in front of a hero. He wanted to be loved by such a man, and he hoped he had inherited some of his strengths.

Durand laughed, as if reading his son's mind. "And yet, my son, I am so very proud of you."

"Of me?" Jourdain looked at him with the crooked smile of a ten-year-old. "But why?"

"Bravery is doing what you must even though it may cost you your life. You fought bravely and strategically, even though the odds were against you."

He looked towards India. "You returned to care for your mother though you had doubts. You are carrying on the family tradition though it is not for the faint-hearted. A lesser man would have fled in fear, yet here you stay. It is I who is proud to have such a son as you."

"I wish I had known you."

"Jourdain, we have little time left for regrets or flowery words, and there are things I must say while I can. I know you wonder what you can expect from this time forward and I'll tell you," his father said. "This land of Langue d'Òc holds ancient secrets in her soul, for long before Christianity developed there were ancient centers within her bosom. Trained Initiates brought the teachings to the villagers through stories, which were in turn written down into books. Once the Vatican took hold, this gnosis was declared heretical. It became necessary for this knowledge to remain hidden, but it has never been lost.

"Like the river that runs underground, invisible through the rocks and ground that hide its path, a stream of knowledge still flows through our Cathar beliefs and sacred books. We are the guardians of the sacred tomes and the Grail, but not their master. The Cathar's physical time on this earth has ended for now, but the knowledge must remain hidden from those who would use its power for ill gain. It is your role to guard all that we hold sacred and to guide those who will come after you so they will continue to seek the truth and remember."

"Not until the passage of seven centuries, in the year of 1944, will the treasure and its knowledge again be sought both by a soul of pure light and a soul of darkness. Our long and proud bloodlines will continue through you until then, when humanity will once again determine whether or not it is worthy and ready for true enlightenment."

The others began to come closer now, as one by one, they laid their hands on his forehead in blessing and in prayer. At the very last was a little girl, with big brown eyes, that smiled and said, "Remember me."

The ghostly features of his parents and the others began to lighten as the mist started to dissipate in gentle swirls. He felt anxious. There were too many questions he needed to ask.

"How will I know who to trust when it's my time to pass this knowledge on?"

The mist continued to dissolve as India looked to him and smiled. "You'll know her when you see her. That I promise. Remember, my son, the Grail takes care of its own."

Only a faint misty image now remained, and he watched in silence as the group turned and walked hand in hand towards the image of a fire where the wooden cross stood. Briefly, turning once, they looked at him, lifted their chins and smiled. Then, hand in hand, they walked together into the center of the fire.

As their figures blended with the flames, tiny random sparks of light blinked through the mist and then slowly increased in number and intensity until, in a final crescendo, they exploded, showering the night sky in a glorious burst of light.

Jourdain stood unable to move in awe and amazement. Not until a distant herd of goats disturbed the wind-swept spell with their bleating and tinkling bells did he look up towards the moonlit summit.

Until we meet again, he thought.

Nodding his head in deep respect, he turned and walked away. Tomorrow, at first light, his journey would begin toward the northwest in search of a secret cave that had been painted like the night sky.

Kate Riley

Epilogue

10 years later
Langue d'óc

It was a perfect summer morning with not a cloud in the sky and the air still fresh from a light rain the night before. Jourdain and his young daughter walked side-by-side along the meadow's path. He stopped to take in a deep breath. There was a certain scent that hung from the earth at these ancient sites that he loved.

His daughter ran on ahead, and he watched her with a smile and a sense of wonderment at his own joy. Sadly, her birth had cost him his wife, but although there were times when he missed Maura, his life had taken a far different turn, one where she could not have followed. He understood that now.

Leo was a strong young man, and had easily taken over the business, married and had already given him a grandchild. And there was his little India. It was indeed a miracle.

The leaves and grass were damp and heavy with dew, and although he frowned on his daughter running around in bare feet, he couldn't deny her the joy of wiggling her toes in the soft grass. As she skipped alongside him, they approached the hill, and his hand reached for hers as it always did, and he said what he always said.

"Here, take my hand so you don't fall."

"You mean so you won't fall."

"Ah! You've found me out."

"Papa, how old are you?"

He smiled. "I am old enough. How old are you?"

"Eight, silly, you already know that. Are you as old as the hills?"

"No, not older than the hills, nor the stars, nor the moon either. Hush and listen. The morning wants to say hello to you."

She stopped and listened, as instructed, then squinted her eyes and grinned a toothless smile.

"That's just the birds." Grabbing his one hand with both of hers, she swung around to face him. "When can I learn to read Greek, Papa?"

"Not until you've mastered Latin. "

"But I already know all the verbs and tenses. You said so yourself."

"What I said was that you were coming along nicely, and that soon we can start with some Greek pages. Remember, this is our secret."

She rolled her eyes and tilted her head. "Yes, Papa. I already know. Little girls are not supposed to know how to read. But I still think it's a foolish rule."

Finally, they reached the top, and he stopped to catch his breath. He eyed his vegetable patch with pride.

"What do you think of my garden today, little one?"

"Your plants look very, very happy, Papa."

He nodded in agreement and smiled into her deep blue eyes. "I think so, too. Shall we see if there are any beans to pick for our stew?"

"All right, but can I check my squash plants first? Yesterday they had flowers."

"Of course, I'll be over here."

Sauntering over to a large patch of vines that wound themselves around a loose wicker screen, he gently brushed aside leaves in order to access the long purple pods. He was in luck, for there were plenty that were just right for tonight's dinner.

"Papa, come see, come see!"

Jourdain looked back at his daughter and laughed.

"What have you found now, ma petite? A gigantic snail? A little fairy? Or perhaps a beautiful unicorn?"

"No, silly, I found a treasure. Come see. Tell me what it is."

"A treasure, eh? Give me a moment, and I'll be right there."

She had already covered half the distance by the time he had even stood up. Her little hands, filthy with dirt, cradled something. What manner of bird or animal had she managed to rescue now?

"Let's have a look then. What have you found?"

"It's the carving of a dove on a cross. Look."

"So it is."

Someone with a clever hand had carved a wooden cross with four equal arms and in the center had inlaid an ivory dove flying over a mountain. At the top, a thin wire had been looped and threaded back into the wood. A broken thin strip of leather had once served to hang it around someone's neck.

"What is it, Papa?"

"It looks to me like a Cathar cross."

"You mean a Cathar, like my Grand-mère India?"

"Yes, exactly like your Grand-mère."

"Can I keep it? Do you think she sent me this for me to find?"

He looked around and shivered in spite of the heat as a subtle breeze caressed his cheek. "I have no doubts that she did, and when we get home I have a very special piece of string to tie through the loop."

"I'm going to wear it always, and when I have a daughter, I'll give it to her to wear, and she in turn, will give it to her daughter after that. That way we will always remember. Don't you think that's a good idea, Papa?"

"I think it's an excellent idea." He smiled and gave her a little side look. "You know, now that I think about it, perhaps you are ready to study some Greek."

"Will you tell me more about Grand-mère as well?"

"I will indeed."

As they began to head back home, Jourdain looked into the deep blue eyes of his successor and placed his hand on the curve of her shoulder where she, too, had been born with the Merovingian birthmark.

THE END

About the Author

Kate Riley is a professional business coach, facilitator and artist who is passionate about the 13th century. Her historical interest in this period was borne from an intense dream where she found herself in a besieged fortress disguised as a young man, surrounded by Templars and about to die. A voice strongly directed her several times to wake up and write down the word 'Cathar'. This dream began a twenty-year obsession, which has twice taken her to Montségur and became the basis for this story.

Ms. Riley's career has encompassed twenty years in the newspaper industry where she has won awards for her designs. She currently lives in a small town north of Toronto, Ontario and manages entrepreneurship programs for adults and youth.

Author Contacts:

Facebook: Kate Riley
https://www.facebook.com/pages/Kate-Riley/1704834233070805?fref=ts

Facebook: The Last Cathar
https://www.facebook.com/thelastcatharbook?fref=ts
Thelastcathar@gmail.com
www.katerileyauthor.ca